A Bargainomics

A
Boatload
OF TROUBLE

Judy Woodward Bates,
a.k.a. The Bargainomics Lady

BARGAINOMICS PUBLICATIONS

A Boatload of Trouble
By Judy Woodward Bates
First Edition, ©2021 by Judy Woodward Bates
All Rights Reserved

ISBN: 978-0-9766166-4-1
Also available in eBook
Bargainomics Publications
Birmingham, AL

Cover Photo: Larry W. Bates
Cover Concept: Judy Woodward Bates
Cover Design & Publishing assistant: The Author's Mentor, www.TheAuthorsMentor.com
Editing & Proofing: Sammie Jo Barstow, www.WatalulaPages.com
Author photo: Larry W. Bates

The following is a work of fiction. Names, characters, places, and incidents are fictitious or used fictitiously. Any resemblance to real persons, living or dead, to factual events, or to businesses is coincidental and unintentional, except where noted in the Acknowledgments and "What's Real?"

Galatians 3:28 in Chapter 9 is quoted from the King James Version of the Holy Bible. Psalm 89:1b in the Dedication is quoted from the Good News Translation of the Holy Bible.

PUBLISHED IN THE UNITED STATES OF AMERICA

DEDICATION

To my Lord and Savior, Jesus Christ.
"I will proclaim your faithfulness forever"
(Psalm 89:1b).

And to my mother, Sybil Willis Woodward,
for teaching me to love words and reading.

Also by Judy Woodward Bates

The Gospel Truth about Money Management
Blessedly Budgeted Women's Events
Bargainomics: Money Management by the Book
The Book of Revelation Unlocked: An Easy-to-Understand Walk
Through the Bible's Final Message

The Bargainomics Lady Mystery Series
A Bargain to Die For
A Boatload of Trouble

ACKNOWLEDGMENTS

Thank you to all the readers of *A Bargain to Die For*. Your positive comments and encouragement made this second mystery possible. Congrats and thank you to Faye Busby, the reader who won the contest to be a character in my next book—she's included in this one. Thank you to Ellen Sallas for her amazing gift for designing the perfect cover, layout, and so much of what makes this book the attractive volume you now hold in your hand or see on your screen. Thank you to my friend, writing retreat pal, and editing and proofing genius Sammie Jo Barstow for her invaluable work on getting my manuscript ready for publication.

Hugs and kisses to my sweet husband Larry who encourages me, understands me, and puts up with my absences in mind and, sometimes, body during my writing binges. Adam Lyle, Larry's niece's husband, deserves a big "Thank you!" for explaining what I needed to know about wreckers.

I so appreciate all the folks at WBRC Fox6 TV in Birmingham, Alabama, who gave me the privilege of many wonderful years of guest spots on their morning show and midday news programs. They are my inspiration for WEEE, the imaginary TV station in this series.

And I could never give enough thanks and praise to my Lord and Savior Jesus Christ. He is my Comforter and Guide. I am so grateful for His love, grace, and mercy, and for the wonderful parents He chose to bring me into this world and teach me about His faithfulness.

A Note from the Author

This is the second book in the Bargainomics Lady Mystery series. The first, *A Bargain to Die For*, included characters—some of whom are mentioned in this second adventure—I decided deserved their stories being told in more detail.

For that reason, I've begun work on non-mystery series which includes Carrie Parker and many of the other endearing folks from *A Bargain to Die For*. We'll follow their lives in *Life in Chalybeate Springs*, the first in my upcoming Chalybeate Springs series. I hope you'll watch for it.

A Bargainomics Lady Mystery • *Book 2*

A
Boatload
OF TROUBLE

1

Summer had been action-packed, to say the least. My cousin Millie and I had made a new friend in folk potter Carrie Parker. Carrie's daughter and son-in-law had both been murdered, although, sadly, divers were never able to recover her daughter's body. Carrie had ended up with custody of her three adorable grandchildren, and, amidst all that, she had received a financial boon that had made her life, and that of her grandchildren, much easier. Knowing Millie and I had had at least a small part in finding the murderer and helping Carrie had been tremendously rewarding.

Still, having come close to death ourselves, Millie and I hoped the next few months would be uneventful. Which is precisely why finding dead bodies was never in the plans for our lakeside getaway. But I'm getting ahead of myself.

The whole thing began with a phone call from my sweet, older friend, Jane Adderly. Knowing how much I appreciate a bargain, she had called me from Plettenberg Bay, South Africa, where she and her husband Cliff were visiting her sister and brother-in-law, and made me an irresistible offer: clean her lake house and get it ready for her family's annual Labor Day party and, in exchange, it was mine to enjoy for one full week. Jane could certainly have afforded to pay a cleaning service—which she usually did—but she knew I wouldn't mind the work and would love the lake time.

I jumped at the opportunity. I'd have to be back at the station the Thursday before the party, but that would work out perfectly. If I hustled on up there, I and the lucky person or persons who went with me would have the place to ourselves for seven whole days. When I'd asked my semi-retired husband Larry about going, he'd politely bowed out, having committed himself to several church and community projects, plus his regular part-time job at Terrell's Classic Garage, where rusted '55 Chevys limped in and rolled out looking better than showroom new.

Millie, a wonderful artist, spent less than a "Millie-second" before agreeing to go with me, and her husband Bill had assured her he'd manage at home just fine without her. Her studio was "open by chance or appointment," so for the next week, it would be closed.

Years ago, she'd taken a 400-square-foot sharecropper's cabin on the old family farm and transformed it into "Millicent's Studio," where she created amazing art from paintings to pottery. In spite of her sporadic hours of business, an impressive number of customers made the drive to Millie's workplace. Art in the Park on Birmingham's Southside and a couple other local galleries kept

2

up a steady demand for her pieces.

Fast forward to the day we're to go to Jane's lake house. As I buzzed along Highway 78, the *William Tell* Overture, or the Lone Ranger's theme song, as many people think of it, interrupted the Terri Blackstock audiobook pouring from my speakers. I quickly hit the answer button on my steering wheel. It was Millie.

"Judy," she chided, "I thought you said you'd be here at 9:15."

"Nooooo," I responded, wondering how many times I'd been through this conversation with my dear cousin. "I said I'd try to leave the station about 9:15, and it's 9:30 now. I'll be there shortly."

"I'll go ahead and carry my stuff out to the end of the driveway. I'll be waiting." I disconnected the call, smiling at the excitement in her voice. Even though I was well into my 50s and Millie had just moved into the next decade, we still loved our girl time as much as we had when we were kids.

The station I'd referred to is WEEE, the oldest TV station in Birmingham, Alabama where I, Judy Woodward Bates, also known as the Bargainomics Lady, have fun sharing money-saving tips during my segments on their morning show, *It's a New Day, Alabama!*, and on the midday news. To clarify, the news segments were every Thursday. I only appeared on the morning show the first and third Thursdays of each month.

Today, though, was the fourth Thursday of the month, which meant no morning show segment. However, the morning show and midday news producers, in a rare moment of kindness, had agreed to let me dash in and prerecord today's midday news segment, plus the morning show segment for the following Thursday, as soon as the morning show wrapped. Ever the sweetheart, my buddy Mickey, the news co-anchor, delayed his between-shows trip to the gym long enough to record the segments with me.

With my five minutes of stardom in the can, as they say in show biz, I was en route to pick up Millie for our stay on beautiful Lewis Smith Lake, a manmade reservoir with more than 550 miles of shoreline stretching over parts of three Alabama counties.

After getting off the highway, I twisted and turned through a half dozen backroads until I saw the "Millicent" sign and the Caffees' funky-looking mailbox, an overall-clad figurine with a mailbox head sporting a patch of green grass "hair." Millie created it as a nod to Papa, our carpenter grandfather, but most people don't know that—they just find it either weird or wonderful.

Their pig trail of a driveway was barely visible through the over-burgeoning natural and added flora, but Millie was already standing by the mailbox, a small piece of luggage and her usual tote bag of art supplies on the ground beside her. I eased into the drive, hopped out, and popped the hatch on my Hyundai Ioniq— my Honda Fit and I had parted company after 12 happy years together. With the back seats down, Millie and I had been known to bring home yard sale deals that some people couldn't fit into a U-Haul. We'd already started learning to pack out the Hyundai. It was all a matter of organization. And we were pros.

"I can't believe we're getting to do this!" Millie fairly

squealed as we threw her bags into the back. "I just hope we can get all the housework done today so we can loaf the rest of the time."

"Today, my foot," I retorted. "If you take the upstairs and I take the downstairs, we should be able to finish the inside in three or four hours. I want some time out on the lake today, and I bet we'll manage it. It won't be dark until 7:30 or so. And before I forget, Jane said her yard man would be coming early next week.

"Oh, and we can clean the porches tomorrow," I added. "It's a big house, but we shouldn't have too tough a job. Knowing Jane, everything was left spotless the last time they were up there."

"Yeah, but how long has that been?" Millie questioned.

"She said they were there for the Fourth of July, so that's only been six or seven weeks. She and Cliff are in South Africa right now, but they'll be back next Thursday and will drive to the lake Friday morning. No worries. We'll have the whole place shipshape in no time. Other than the beds we sleep in, we'll put on the fresh linens the day before we leave. And we'll throw our beds' linens in the wash as soon as we get up on our last day. That way, everything'll be nice and clean."

While some parts of the lake were only a few minutes from the interstate, Jane's place was in Swallow Point, a remote area adjoining the Bankhead National Forest. Having been to Jane's before, I knew we'd better make sure we were taking everything we'd need. It was a good 20-minute drive back to Orville's One-Stop, a combination gas station, grocery, and sandwich shop. Anything with a bigger selection than Orville's meant a 45-minute excursion into Fall Creek.

As I drove, Millie and I discussed what to pick up at the Super Center. By the time we reached Fall Creek, Millie had made a list and divided it between the two of us.

"You'll get all the refrigerated and freezer goods, and I'll grab the rest," Millie ordered, handing me my half of the list. Climbing out and heading to the store entrance, we checked our phones and agreed to meet in 15 minutes. Like I said earlier, we both are pros.

By 10:30 we were through the checkout and out the door. "Hang on a sec," I said, pointing to the food truck by the sidewalk. "Let's grab some sandwiches and take them with us. We can put away the groceries, enjoy our lunch, and get started cleaning."

"Sounds good to me," Millie agreed. We scanned the menu, spotted a two-for-one special, and ordered it: chicken salad sandwiches with chips, a dill pickle spear, and the cookie of your choice—we both opted for white chocolate Macadamia.

Packing our purchases in and around the cooler I'd stored in the hatch, we hit the road again and, with a few minutes to spare before 11:30, turned into Jane's long, winding driveway. As we cleared the natural woodland that opened onto Jane's front lawn, a magnificent vista opened before us.

"Wow!" Millie exclaimed. "When you told me about this

place, you didn't come close to doing it justice."

While Millie was a first-time visitor, I'd been to Jane's lake house a number of times, and it most definitely was a beauty: a rustic stone and cedar two-story with an almost level oak-covered lawn that abruptly halted where a sheer rock wall plunged straight down into the clear blue water. There, at the water's edge, the water level fluctuated between 40 and 50 feet deep, but it was purported to be close to 200 feet deep in areas closer to the hydroelectric dam.

"Let's at least walk down to the water first," Millie suggested. And that we did.

With the lake's fluctuations in water level, piers and boathouses were all on floats, and walkways could be let out or brought in as needed. In the case of Jane's place, the walkway to her boathouse led to a rooftop sun deck, and a set of stairs led from the deck down to the two boat slips beneath and to the connected open swim pier. A substantial pontoon boat took up one slip while a small aluminum fishing boat on the other side hardly took up any space at all. The outer corner away from the swim pier had been enclosed into a storage area where Jane had said we'd find life jackets and other water-related necessities. A black plastic platform floated alongside the swim pier with a pair of colorful Sea-Doos resting in place.

"Ooooh," Millie breathed. "Do we have the use of any of these water toys?"

"Every one of them," I assured her. "Jane told me where all

7

the keys are kept and said to 'use them like they're your own.' I plan to."

"How about we eat out here?" I suggested. "I don't want to be indoors any longer than we have to be."

"Perfect," Millie agreed. "Let's get the car unloaded and get going. Do you have the key?"

"No, Jane said they leave one here. There's a plastic case with a set of barbecue tools in the cabinet under the grill. It's inside the case. When you get the house unlocked, go in and open the garage door. The car will stay cooler if I park in there, and we won't have so far to carry everything."

It took a couple trips each to bring everything inside, and we barely took time to look around as we tossed items onto the counter or into the fridge or freezer. There'd be time to ooh and aah after we'd had our picnic.

Minutes later, we had raised the umbrella on a well-anchored table and bench set on the sun deck and were munching sandwiches and admiring the scenery. Aside from bird calls and the occasional splash of a jumping fish, there was only the sighing of a soft breeze through the trees.

And our own sighs. "This is heaven," I announced.

"Here, here," Millie seconded. "We just got here and I'm already wishing we could stay longer."

"And then there's that nasty little thing called reality," I said. "Let's just be thankful for the time we'll have."

Crumpling her paper and licking the last of the potato chip

grease from her fingers, Millie declared, "I've got to at least get a toe in the water. Then I will willingly become the housemaid."

Temps were already hitting the 90s and today was promising to be a scorcher. "I think I'll join you," I said, swiping at the beads of sweat on my forehead. "Good thing we turned the A/C on before we came out here. The house should be a good bit cooler by the time we walk back up."

Unlike the murky greenish-brown water where our families' cabins had been on the river, Smith's waters ranged from blue to blue-green and, here, was clear enough to see what color toenail polish we were wearing. A few minutes dangling our feet from the swim pier and we were ready to knock out that housework and hurry back to the water.

From the garage, we'd hauled our stuff through a sort of combination mud room, laundry room, pantry, and storage room. The right inner wall was lined with cabinets and open shelving while the outer wall was covered in large hooks where fishing equipment, skis, and other water toys were hanging. The washer, dryer, and an upright freezer stood against the wall that adjoined the kitchen.

And what a kitchen! It was sunny and high-ceilinged, with two walls of white-painted, glass-front cabinets above what appeared to be teakwood countertops. Between the upper and lower cabinetry on the left wall, a solid bank of windows offered an unobstructed view of the lawn, boathouse, and lake. A big copper farmhouse sink complemented the collection of copper cookware suspended from a rack over the center island while the right-hand wall included the fridge, microwave, a gas cooktop, and a separate built-in double oven.

Straight out from the kitchen, the open living and dining area stretched the full depth of the house, with three pairs of French doors opening onto a screened porch facing the water. Like most lake houses, the "front" door that faced the distant roadway was probably rarely used since the focus of everything was the lakeside.

Just off the living/dining area, around the corner from the kitchen, a short hallway included the door to a full bath on the left and guest bedroom door at the end. Across from the living/dining area, a master bedroom and bath took up the other end of the main level, with another pair of French doors opening onto the porch.

"Why don't we draw straws to see who gets to sleep in here?" Millie suggested, running a hand over the matelassé bedspread in the master bedroom.

"You can have it," I said. "I don't care where I sleep. I'll take the other bedroom down here. There's a separate A/C unit for the second level, so we'll turn it off after you finish cleaning up there. No sense running both units since we won't be using the upstairs."

"You won't get any argument out of me," Millie responded. She ducked out of the room and returned with her bags.

"I'll strip the two beds down here and get the first laundry load going," I announced.

"I'll head on upstairs," Millie said. "Didn't I see a vacuum

10

cleaner by the dryer?"

"Yep," I answered. "Help yourself, and the cabinet beside it is loaded with all the cleaning products we'll need. As soon as I start the washer, I'll get to work on the downstairs bathrooms."

"Okey-doke," Millie responded.

While she tackled the four bedrooms and two baths upstairs, I gave both downstairs baths a good cleaning, then changed out laundry loads before moving into the kitchen. I pulled my phone from the hip pocket of my denim Bermuda shorts and checked the time. At this pace, we were going to have plenty of play time.

Two hours later, Millie came downstairs lugging the vacuum cleaner and presented it to me. "Here," she said. "I'm done with the vacuuming and dusting. I'll dust everything again before we leave. We are staying until next Thursday, aren't we?"

"Yes," I answered. My TV segment info had to be submitted and approved at least two days in advance, so I explained, "Jane has Wi-Fi. I can submit my info and graphics to the station from here, and I brought an outfit to wear, so we can drive straight to WEEE. And since I was able to prerecord the morning show segment, I won't have to be there until shortly before the noon news. Then I'll buy you lunch and take you home after that."

"Deal," Millie said, and tromped back up the stairs to finish her cleaning.

After barely more than another hour, the house was spit-shined; the downstairs beds were remade with fresh bedding; and Millie had stripped all the upstairs beds and delivered their linens

11

to the laundry room. "We'll take care of all this Wednesday evening so the downstairs beds will be all we have to worry with Thursday morning," she explained. "You probably had the worst of it since the downstairs gets more use than the second floor."

"No, it wasn't bad at all," I said, "except for the second bedroom and bathroom down here. That bed hadn't been made and there were a couple dirty towels on the floor and a washcloth hung over the shower curtain rod. For some reason, Jane, or whoever checked the house before they left last time, missed those two rooms."

"Could be they had a late leaver," Millie suggested. "Especially if it was a grandkid, they might not have bothered to tidy up before they went out the door."

"I bet that's it," I said, "and that probably explains the dirty plate and cup I found in the sink. Everything else was in perfect order."

"I guess when you've got a houseful of people and you're trying to get everyone and everything out the door, it's easy to miss a spot," Millie said, "but it sounds more like a straggler who didn't clean up after himself."

"Yeah," I conceded. "Now how about that water?"

2

In a matter of minutes, we were in swimsuits and had thrown sunscreen and towels into a bag to take with us. "Let's grab some bottles of water too," I suggested. We snagged the water and a few snacks and left through the side door.

I passed Millie a Sea-Doo key on a floating key chain and opened the seat of one Sea-Doo to stuff in my towel, sunscreen, water, and snacks. Millie followed suit with the other. After I unlocked the cable that secured the Sea-Doos in place, we climbed aboard our water toys and gently rocked them until they slipped off their platform. Then we were off.

Weekdays after school is back in session is a great time to be on the lake. Minimal boat traffic. Rarely choppy water. We'd have a smooth ride to anywhere we wanted to go. And since I knew this part of the lake very well, I was sure we could cover a lot of ground and still be back before even the beginning of dusk.

After we'd traveled a little distance, I felt more confident and started performing a few easy antics, like circling in front of Millie and then gunning the Sea-Doo to give her a good spray as I shot by.

"Hey!" she yelled. "Two can play that game!" Two not-so-young grownups were behaving like teenagers. And loving it.

After we tired of spraying each other and acting goofy, I led the way to a narrow inlet and slowed to a crawl so Millie could pull up beside me. "Wanted to show you this," I said, as we puttered around a curve and entered a circular opening with 20-foot high rock cliffs towering above it. A dainty waterfall cascaded down the back of the tiny cove.

"It's like what you see in a commercial for some tropical island," Millie whispered. "It's too pretty for words."

"I know. Larry and I have ridden back here a lot of times." For several years, he and I have kept an RV at Harvey's Marina, along with our own pair of Sea-Doos. For now, though, sweet Jane had supplied us with everything we could wish for.

"I bet that's not all you and Larry have done back here," Millie said with a grin.

"That," my dear cousin, "is none of your beeswax," I responded. "I am not a woman who'll kiss and tell."

"What's that over there?" Millie interrupted, pointing to a large grayish shape beneath the waterfall.

"Probably one of those big carp," I said. "They get enormous."

Barely touching the throttle, I putted toward the cascade to get a better look. "Omigosh," I blurted. "It's a body." The gray t-shirt

14

Millie had spotted had formed an air pocket, and the rest of the body dangled beneath like the tentacles of a bizarre giant jellyfish.

Standing and flipping open the seat of her Sea-Doo, Millie grabbed her phone and punched in 9-1-1. "We need to report a drowning victim," Millie spoke into the phone. "Let me let you speak to my cousin. She knows the area better than I do."

"She wants to know where we are," Millie said, passing her phone to me.

I gave the best possible description of our location. "We're in the Make-Out Cove. No, we didn't attempt CPR. This person appears to have been here a while. Yes, we'll stay with the body. But, please, get someone here quick. We don't want to be out here when it gets dark."

"The Make-Out Cove?" Millie asked. "That's the name of this place?"

"Not officially," I said, "but it's one of the worst-kept secrets on the lake. If you're a regular laker, you've probably been here."

Place names often hinted or blatantly announced what the area was known for, as in Gobbler's Knob, where turkey hunters used to say the turkeys were as thick as mosquitoes, and Panther Creek, where mountain lions were abundant back when that valley was settled.

In Caufield Corner, the unincorporated spot in the road where Larry and I lived, the best landmark to tell anyone where to turn off the highway was the Booby Barn, a topless bar in a prime location right before the change from Jefferson County to Walker.

At a wedding reception, an acquaintance was asking me where we lived. In explanation, I gave the usual instructions, "You turn off at the Booby Barn."

"I heard that," came the voice of my pastor, grinning.

"Well, you tell me a better landmark, and I'll start using it," I said. I had him stumped on that one.

"Is it a man or a woman?" Millie asked, pulling me out of my thoughts and back to the elephant in the room.

"I think it's a man," I said, "but if you want to know anything else, you can do the examining yourself. I just want to sit here and pretend like there isn't a dead body in the water with us."

The wail of sirens grew louder and louder and then stopped. We heard the slamming of doors, and a minute or two later, two EMTs and four police officers appeared at the top of the waterfall. Simultaneously, the Marine Police idled into the cove.

"Ladies," one of the Marine Police said, "if you'll move your Sea-Doos to the mouth of the cove and wait, we'll need to ask you a few questions."

The land cops, frustrated that the Marine Police were getting first dibs, began making their way down the slippery rocks along the edge of the falls. Despite the grave circumstances, the Keystone Cops came to mind as the third officer slipped, slammed into the one in front of him, and landed the frontrunner in the brink. The fourth guy—or gal, in her case—never cracked a grin as she picked her way to the bottom.

"What have we got here?" the female asked, addressing the

Marine officer while two of her colleagues hauled the third one out of the water.

"Tell you in a second," he responded, giving a nod to the wetsuit-clad officer who was with him. We watched as Wetsuit dropped smoothly into the water and swam to the body.

"Male, maybe in his early 30s, t-shirt and shorts. No shoes. Could have been wearing sandals. If so, we may find them floating nearby. Most likely, he fell from up there," Wetsuit said, pointing above the falls. "Lotta folks want to get too close a view and end up in the water. Only this guy must have hit the rocks on the way down."

Millie and I gave each other a look. If there'd been any evidence to show where the man had originally landed, the trio's downhill slide had done away with it.

Another door slammed and a petite, dark-skinned woman was soon peering down from the bluff. "I see you fellas had some problems getting down there," she called, eyeing the wet and muddy threesome. "If I could get some assistance, I'd prefer an easier method."

"Who's that?" I asked Marine Police One, who finally introduced himself as Officer Jackson.

"Doc Okada. She's the coroner. And a GP at the clinic over in Fall Creek," he added.

The two EMTs secured a knotted rope to a substantial tree atop the bluff, and used it to assist themselves and the doc down to the now crowded narrow rock shelf that stood at water level. "Bring the body over here," Doc called to Wetsuit.

Wetsuit complied, carefully towing the floating body to the ledge, where the EMTs hoisted him onto the rock and rolled him over. Millie and I closed our eyes, but curiosity had us both peeking in a matter of seconds.

"Nasty," Doc said. "He took a major blow to the parietal."

"In English," Jackson requested.

"The back of his skull got smashed."

"That I can understand," Jackson said. "Like Osgood said, he probably got too close to the edge and took a nosedive."

"Possibly," Doc said. "Or he was pushed. Or was never up there in the first place. He may have been injured or killed elsewhere and his body simply drifted into the cove."

"Are you saying you suspect foul play?" one of the muddy officers asked.

"I'm saying," said the doc, "that, at this point, I wouldn't discount his having been dropped from an alien aircraft. I'll need to get him to the morgue before I can tell you anything definitive."

And that was that. Officer Wetsuit, a.k.a. Osgood, climbed back aboard the patrol boat, and Jackson asked me and Millie to tie off to the boat and come aboard to make our statements. As we did so, Jackson popped the familiar question.

"Aren't you that Bargain Lady on TV?" he asked.

"Bargainomics Lady," I corrected. "That's me."

"My wife watches you all the time," he said.

It always amazes me how many men recognize me because

their wives are viewers. I mean, if Larry sees a sunrise, do I, by osmosis, absorb the same experience? Just saying.

"Well, tell her I said, 'Hi,' and that I wish I'd met you under better circumstances."

We watched as the body was bagged and a board lowered to the ledge. The black bundle was strapped to the board and hauled up the cliff side, one EMT guiding from the top and the other carefully controlling his gruesome cargo as it glided up the wall. Behind him, the four policemen wisely used the EMTs' rope to aid their ascent.

Millie and I weren't exactly a barrelful of enlightenment, so it didn't take long for Jackson to take our statements, get our contact info, and send us on our way. From phone call to finish, the whole ordeal had taken less than two hours. We still had some time before dark.

A subdued duo cruised back toward Jane's, waving back at a friendly couple fishing off their dock. If only they knew what had happened so close to their peaceful piece of paradise. No doubt, they'd heard the commotion. They'd learn the bad news soon enough.

I pointed out a few of the more spectacular houses along this portion of Smith, and then we were back in the Bankhead Forest with nothing but the water and woods all around us. What normally struck me as natural beauty now felt isolated and sinister. I knew Larry and I would never feel the same about Make-Out Cove. It gave me shivers just to think of the place.

19

Two more houses came into view, and a minute or two later, we had docked the Sea-Doos. "We need to call Larry and Bill," Millie said. "You know they're going to see this on the news."

"Speaking of news," I said, "it's a miracle a news crew didn't get there before they got that body out of there. I need to call the station and make sure they're covering the story."

I ducked into the shade of the boathouse and plopped into a seat on the pontoon. "Newsroom," a male voice answered.

"This is Judy, the Bargainomics Lady." Even after all the years I've been at the station, I had never met some of the night and evening crew. WEEE was a big and scattered family. "Is anyone checking into the body that was just pulled out of Smith Lake?" I asked.

"Melanie Posten's on it," the voice said. "This is JJ, girl. I know who you are, Ms. Bargainomics." JJ had been one of the first to welcome me when I began my segments on WEEE.

"Great," I said. "Wanted to make sure y'all had it covered."

"And how were you on it?" JJ asked. "Come on, who's your contact?"

"I'll tell you when I see you," I promised. "I'll send Melanie a text in the meantime."

"All right, but I'm going to find out who your source is," JJ said. "Even if I have to resort to bribery. I know how much you love your Blizzards."

"You know me too well," I said, laughing. "For a Blizzard, I'll spill the beans about anything. Hope to see you soon."

I fired off a text to Melanie, knowing she'd likely ignore it while she was in the middle of an investigation. "I found lake body," I wrote. "Need details, call me."

Keeping it simple got her attention. One glance and she knew my text could be a gold mine. My phone thrummed the *William Tell* Overture and I answered, "Hi, Mel."

She was in speed mode, so she wasted no time on small talk. "You actually found the body?" she asked. "Give me details."

As quickly as possible, I walked her through the entire event. "How about an on-camera interview?" she asked.

"Not happening," I said. "Unless you want me to talk Bargainomics."

"Not even for me?" she pleaded, playing on our friendship.

"Not even," I said. "But I can tell you information I bet the other reporters won't have."

"Spill it," she said. "I gotta hurry."

I told her about Make-Out Cove and the names of the Marine Police who'd been on the scene. "Osgood," I added, "was the first person to approach the body."

Melanie thanked me profusely, promising, "Lunch is on me next time we get together," before disconnecting.

I had no doubt WEEE would have the most detailed coverage in the business.

"This getaway has sure gotten off to a gruesome start," Millie said. "I'm so tense, I wish Bill was here to give me a back and neck massage."

21

"If that's a hint," I said, "you're wasting your breath. What we need is our own personal masseuse." Which we actually had, in the form of our friend Cheryl. One call, and she, her table, and her magic fingers would be Johnny-on-the-spot.

"I wouldn't ask Cheryl to drive all the way up here," Millie said. "Besides, her regular clients keep her really busy. Maybe we can book an appointment after we're home."

When Cheryl first began her training, she brought her table to our house and asked me and Larry to be guinea pigs. I was an instant "yes," and Larry was a loud and uncompromising "no."

"I'm not letting her put her hands all over me," Larry said, as though Cheryl wasn't standing right there beside us. "And I'm sure not taking off my clothes."

"Good grief," I argued, "if Dr. Weatherby, our regular GP, asked you to undress, would you refuse?"

"Of course not," he said. "She's a doctor."

"And you are a goofball," I said. "Massage therapists are trained professionals, not sex workers. They don't touch you anywhere you'd be uncomfortable being touched. They don't tell you to strip naked. You wear whatever's comfortable for you. And whatever part she's not working on is covered with a sheet. Honestly, Larry Bates, I'm surprised at you."

"Matter of fact," I added, "I should be mad at you. What do you think 'Massages by George' and I were up to when you gave me that gift certificate last Christmas?"

Larry didn't have an answer for that one.

"Cheryl is training to be a massage therapist, not a hooker," I said. "She'll need 650 hours in an accredited school of massage to get her license. If you're her friend, you'll help her."

That last bit did it, and the most reluctant client on earth stripped to his gym shorts and climbed onto Cheryl's table. Five minutes later, the man was putty in her hands. Now, when he twists his back out of whack under one of those classic cars, it's Cheryl to the rescue. He's even made a believer out of Terrell.

"We'll get our Cheryl time in soon after we get home," I told Millie. "Right now, I want to enjoy our getaway. But then, I feel bad about wanting to enjoy myself after what happened to that poor man."

"I know. It sounds so terrible to say I don't want finding that body to put a damper on our time here," Millie said.

"*Damper* may have not been the best choice of words," I said, "but I know what you mean."

We decided on a short swim before going back to the house.

"You know," Millie said, as she floated lazily beside me, "I would love to have a place like this, but I could never stay here by myself. It'd creep me out, not being able to see another house around me. Especially after finding that body."

"The Bollings are your nearest neighbors, and you can't see them from your house," I pointed out.

"True," she said. "I guess I'm just used to that. However," she added, "I'd get used to this if Jane decided to give it to me."

"Oh, but you'd never be alone here, even if Bill was away for weeks on end," I told her. "I mean, we're family. I'd be here for you. Literally."

We both laughed and decided it was time to head in. "What is it about being around water that always makes me so hungry?" I said.

"I don't know," Millie answered, "but it has the same effect on me. Glad we bought that frozen pizza. Let's pop it in the oven and take our showers while it bakes."

"Sounds like a plan," I said.

When we both appeared in the kitchen clean, makeup-less, and wearing sleep shirts, there were only four minutes left on the timer, during which I rounded up plates and paper towels while Millie filled a couple glasses with ice and located the pizza cutter.

"Let's sit on the porch," I suggested. Moments later, we were kicked back in chaise lounges watching the night sky unfurl a blanket of countless winking stars.

"Was that French door hard to open?" I asked, waving a slice of pizza toward the door we'd come through. "I noticed you had to tug on it a little bit. I was afraid you were going to drop your pizza."

"It took a little more pull than I expected. At first, I thought it was still locked, but it wasn't. It just took a little muscle."

"I didn't unlock it. Didn't you unlock it?" I asked, a nervous tickle crawling up my spine.

"No, I thought you'd unlocked it," Millie answered, concern knitting her brow. "We'd better check all the doors before we go

24

to bed tonight."

"And the windows. And the closets. And all the upstairs while we're at it," I said, trying to sound lighthearted. "I know that's probably overkill, but better safe than sorry."

"Good idea," Millie agreed, "but not a good time to use the word 'kill' in any form." She had no idea how right she was.

Mid-way through our pizza, a whippoorwill began its evening serenade. "Oh, listen," Millie said. "Reminds me of when we were kids and would sleep on the porch down at the river."

"Yeah, it does," I said. "But that was then, with a houseful of grownups to protect us. This chicken ain't sleepin' on nobody's porch out here in the middle of nowhere."

"You will always be our family's big baby," Millie chuckled, reminding me I was last place in our first-cousin hierarchy.

After cleaning up the kitchen, we scoured a huge tower of movies and found a great old classic, "Neptune's Daughter," starring Esther Williams and Red Skelton. "Let's watch it in *my* bedroom," Millie suggested, emphasizing her ownership of the master suite.

"But first, we check the doors and windows," I reminded her. Only my bedroom window and one French door proved to have been left unlocked, both of which we quickly remedied and attributed to the late-leaving grandchild. We piled into the king-size bed and popped in the movie.

"Wait," I said before pressing *play*. "We need to see the news report."

"I guess I was trying to block all that out of my mind," Millie said. "Of course, let's watch that first."

The News at Nine had just begun, and I knew Melanie's story would either be the lead-off or be teased big-time at the top of the show. "A Thursday outing on the lake," said anchorman Steve Cofer, "turns to horror when two local women discover a body. Stay with us. Melanie Posten has a full report coming up in a moment."

"She wouldn't!" Millie shrieked. "I don't want the whole world knowing we found that body!"

"Chill," I said. "Melanie won't do that. And there were no news crews there. We're all right."

That seemed to dial down Millie's panic level. We waited through several uninteresting reports until, at last, Melanie stood before the camera. Her chocolatey brown skin was flawless and her hair was piled high in a flattering upswept style. Some people think all that hair might not be hers. But I knew better. Her shoulder-length hair was as real as the auburn spikes on my own head.

Melanie had apparently commandeered a boat before nightfall. "The picturesque scene before me," she said, as the view moved from her to the cascading waterfall, "was being enjoyed by two women out for a ride on their Sea-Doos, when peace turned to panic as one woman spotted a body floating just beneath this waterfall."

"The two called 9-1-1," she continued, "and police, Marine

26

Police, and EMTs were dispatched, along with Dr. Lizzie Okada, the Winston County coroner. Video obtained by WEEE shows the body was moved to a narrow ledge while Dr. Okada performed an initial examination." A fuzzy video of the doc bending over the body played as Melanie narrated.

"Jackson," I said. "Jackson had to have taken that video with his phone. Osgood was in the water, and you and I were the only other people who could have videoed from that angle."

"He better not have videoed us," Millie said, anger tinging her words.

"He didn't," I said. "Even if the producer forced Melanie to use video with us in it, she would have given us a heads-up."

"Better not have," Millie said again.

"According to our sources, this beautiful inset has long been dubbed 'Make-Out Cove' by those familiar with it."

"'Our sources,'" I echoed. "That would be us."

Melanie launched into every detail I'd told her, concluding with new information. "Dr. Okada has declined to speculate on cause of death, but assures us that her autopsy report is forthcoming. Meanwhile, the body has been identified, but the name is being withheld pending notification of the family."

"See," I said, "I knew Melanie would never let us down." I picked up my phone and texted her, "Good segment."

"Have you talked to Bill?" I asked.

"Yes," Millie answered, "I gave him a call right before I jumped in the shower. I didn't want him seeing that news report and being upset about a body being found so close to where we're staying. I assured him we were fine. Creeped out a bit, but fine."

"Right," I said. "It's not like he had a bullet hole through his forehead."

"Hush!" Millie yelped. "I don't even want to think about it."

"I meant he's not a murder victim. He very likely fell, hit his head, and drowned. Sad, but not something to make us think there's a crazed killer on the loose."

"You," Millie deadpanned, "are not using comfort words."

"Let's watch the movie and drop this," I said, taking up the remote. "And before you ask, I've already talked to Larry and told him there was nothing going on up here to worry about."

Three quick notes signaled a text on my phone, so I checked it before starting the movie. It was Melanie. "Thx. Jackson did have your photos. I 'accidentally' deleted them while I was pulling the other photos off his phone. I did sincerely apologize." A winking emoji ended her message.

"You're the best," I texted back.

"Jackson did take our pics," I said.

"He what!" Millie wailed. "I knew it, I knew it! Thank Melanie for not showing them," she said. "Oh, but what if he's sent them to any other media?"

"Didn't happen," I said with confidence. "Melanie got to him first and 'accidentally' deleted the photos of us."

"God bless that sweet woman," Millie said.

"Indeed," I answered.

After tossing around several scenarios about the dead guy, we concluded this was a poor bedtime topic. "Let's just watch the movie," I said. And Millie agreed.

We decided Esther Williams' character Eve and her sister Betty reminded us of ourselves. "You can be Betty," Millie said, "since she's the younger sister." After all, I was six years younger than Millie, an age difference that made me nothing more than a pest in our younger years, but now was something we never gave a thought to, unless, like with the movie, there was something to rib each other about.

Being Betty turned out to be okay, since I ended up with Red Skelton. "But I'd rather have been Eve," I whined, "because she got to marry Ricardo Montalbán."

"You mean José," Millie corrected.

"Whatever," I sniped. "You got the cuter guy."

"But at least we had a nice double wedding," she said, grinning devilishly.

"Just forget it," I said, swinging my feet off the side of the bed. "I'm going to sleep and dream about Ricardo Montalbán. And I hope you dream about Red Skelton."

"Nighty night," Millie responded, fluttering her fingertips in farewell. "If I'm not awake when you serve breakfast, just leave it on the dresser."

"If you're not awake when I make breakfast, I'll be making breakfast for one," I snapped. "Good night." I banged the door shut and huffed across to the other bedroom.

I'd been asleep for an hour or so—my phone showed it was just after midnight—when I heard a scratching sound outside my window. Heart racing, I lay completely still and listened. I heard it again. And then a muffled, "What the ..." followed by what I was sure was the pounding of running feet.

Snatching my door open, I sprinted to Millie's room, sending her bolting upright in a half-sleep stupor, "Wh-what's wrong? What are you doing?"

"Somebody was outside my window! And I think they were trying to get in!"

"I thought you'd grown out of this by now," Millie said in a sleepy but calm voice. "You were having a nightmare. It's not real. Now go back to bed," she added, yawning and groaning.

"I know I confused dreams and reality when I was a *child*," I emphasized, "but that was a long time ago. I was *not* dreaming! I'm telling you, there was somebody out there."

"Well, after all this commotion, I'm sure whoever or whatever it was didn't stick around. Just get in here and let's get some sleep," Millie said, flipping back the covers and patting the unoccupied side of the bed. "It'll all be better in the morning."

That was one thing that really made me fume: how a well-seasoned adult woman could be made to feel like a six-year-old child again just because the 12-year-old never believed me when I told her I'd been surrounded by aliens or robot monsters or other night terrors. Still, I was glad to be sharing Millie's bed. I wouldn't be getting any sleep if I went back to my bedroom.

Millie's quiet breathing told me she was asleep again in no time. I lay awake, listening for other prowler sounds, but hearing only the whippoorwill and the occasional hoot owl. Daylight was peeping through the blinds when I finally nodded off.

3

"Good morning, Sleepy-Head," Millie called all too cheerfully and loudly as I stumbled out onto the porch. "There's a carafe of coffee, some O.J., and bran muffins over there," she said, pointing to a small table under the kitchen window.

"Morning," I mumbled, flopping down on a chaise lounge and rubbing my eyes with my closed fists.

"Stop that!" Millie fussed. "We get enough wrinkles at our age without you grinding in extra ones."

"Yes, Mother," I responded. "Let me rest in silence until I can drag myself over to the table."

"After what you did last night, you hardly deserve silence," Millie reminded me. "You woke me from a lovely dream with Ricardo Montalbán. Now all I have is Hercule Poirot to keep me company," she said, tapping the front of her paperback, "and it's just not the same."

"Personally, I prefer Hercule," I sniffed. "But why am I not surprised that you got to dream about Ricardo? Nobody I wanted to see was in my dreams last night."

"Like your scary burglar?" Millie grinned.

"No," I snapped. "Like that drowned guy. But my burglar was real, and I'll prove it as soon as I've had a glass of tea and a muffin."

"What, no coffee?" Millie questioned.

"Not in this weather. I'm starting off with a cold drink."

I returned from the kitchen with a tall glass of iced tea and plucked a muffin off the table on my way by. Back in my chaise lounge, I stared out at the shimmering water.

"What say we take the pontoon out and go around to Rock Ledge Marina and feed the fish?"

"Sounds like fun," Millie agreed. Larry and I had made countless trips to Rock Ledge where the floating store and gas station sold snacks for people, plus saltine crackers to feed the giant carp that had made their home there.

"Let's put a picnic lunch together and take our books with us," Millie suggested. "What'd you bring with you?"

"I couldn't make up my mind, so I brought a selection," I said.

"Mysteries, of course," Millie nodded.

"Yep. I just put Sheri Cobb South's latest John Pickett mystery on my tablet, and I brought along Barbara Hambly's *Murder in July*. I don't know how I let myself get so far behind on this series. I was hooked after I read the first one, *A Free Man of Color*."

"That's about Benjamin January in early New Orleans, isn't

it?" Millie asked. "I'd forgotten about him."

"That's the guy. I think Hambly's books should be required reading for Black History Month. They may be murder mysteries, but they're historically accurate and I learn something new every time I read one."

"Aren't the John Pickett mysteries historic, too?" Millie asked. "I seem to recall he's some sort of policeman in London, isn't he?"

"Yeah, and he falls for a lady way above his class," I explained. "But if you haven't read them, that's all I'm telling you. Is that the only book you brought with you?" I asked, giving a nod toward her paperback. Millie isn't the avid reader that I am.

Reaching down into the tote on the floor beside her, she hauled out two bulky volumes and held them up for me to see. "Two books on water painting techniques."

"Watercolors?" I asked.

"No, painting water, as in this lake," she said, waving a hand toward the shoreline, "or the ocean, or even a glass of water. Water can be tricky to draw and paint. And I'm always interested in new techniques and ideas."

Since my artistic ability was limited to making Play-Doh worms, I changed to a subject more in my wheelhouse. "I did have a couple of my photos mounted on canvas," I said. I hung them in the breakfast room. They're the closest thing to 'art' I'll ever do."

"That is art," Millie insisted. "And I have no doubt you put your Bargainomics brain to work on finding the best deal on the canvases."

"Seventy percent off during a one-day sale," I smiled. "If finding bargains is an art, just call me Michelangelo."

In my bathroom, I slipped into a swimsuit and slathered myself with waterproof sunscreen before throwing on a short beach-themed dress as a cover-up. Rounding up my "Sea U Later" ball cap, I dropped it and my sunglasses into my tote, along with my tablet and my Barbara Hambly whodunit.

Millie was already similarly dressed and slapping mayo onto some multigrain bread for our sandwiches. "Here," she said, pointing her knife toward the sink. "I've already washed that tomato. Slice it and put it in a container. We don't want our sandwiches to get soggy. Tomato and mayo suit you?"

"If that tomato's out of Bill's garden, it sure does. I've got some grapes in the freezer. We can take those along. And did I mention I brought brownies?"

"You had me at frozen grapes," Millie answered. "But brownies definitely work for me too. What kind?"

"Cream cheese with pecans," I answered. "Care for a sample?"

"Tempting, but no," Millie said. "I want my first bite to be over water. I am so looking forward to getting back out on the lake."

We found a wagon in the laundry room and loaded it with our bags and cooler, and rolled it out to the deck and down the short ramp to the driveway. "Do you have the house and boat keys?" Millie asked.

"Yes'm," I said, holding aloft a small keyring and shaking it. "And before you ask, yes, they float." I pointed out the key ring's miniature red and white buoy. "But first, we're going around front and let me show you where the burglar was last night."

"Oh, right," Millie said, rolling her eyes.

"You know I hate it when you do that," I reminded her. "Come on."

We trudged around the corner, me in the lead. As we reached the area near the bedroom window, I held up my hand as a "halt" signal and started scanning the ground for telltale footprints. It'd been too dry. My night visitor hadn't left a single clue.

"Are you satisfied now, nightmare queen?" Millie asked, hands on hips. "See, no broken twigs in the shrubbery. Nothing. Just as I figured."

"Fine," I said, "but I promise you that was no dream. Somebody was out here last night."

"Whatever," said Millie, waving off my nighttime visitor just as she always had. "Let's forget this and go have some fun."

Which is what we did. Millie unlocked the chain, tossed in the ropes, and climbed aboard as I backed the pontoon out of its slip and pointed us toward open water. I was glad the top was already up on the boat because this redhead's pale white skin could easily burn in the shade. Sunscreen and I were together year-round, thanks to the long line of Celtic genes my mother had so generously shared with me.

Millie, on the other hand, took after her mom's and my dad's side of the family—her mom and my dad were siblings. In the dead of winter, her skin was a pretty shade of tan. In summer, she would turn as brown as a bean.

Oh, and Millie was not only my cousin and bestie. She was also my Vanna White, helping me with my show 'n' tell items and occasionally modeling for me at my speaking engagements. I'll explain more about that later.

Anyway, several years ago, she scared us all with a cancer diagnosis that meant both radiation and chemotherapy. When her baby fine, straight, dark hair departed, the new batch came in lusciously thick and platinum silver. She was a trouper, and has been cancer-free long enough that her oncologist has now reduced her visits to only annual checkups. Bigger-boned and a whole inch taller than my five foot two, Millie is what many people would call a strikingly handsome woman. I, on the other hand, am redheaded, scrawny, pale, and, I suppose, decent-looking, or they wouldn't let me on television.

When we cruised back by the heavy woods of the Bankhead,

I spotted a dark object bobbing in the water. I eased the throttle back as a second object appeared a few feet from the first one. "Hey, those are divers," I said. "That's really dangerous, being out there with no dive flag out."

The two divers continued to float on the surface as I drew the pontoon nearer. "Hey!" I yelled. "Are y'all all right?"

The much stockier-looking one of the pair turned and grinned, offering a thumbs-up. "We're good!" he yelled back. He took a swipe at his shoulder length dark hair, pushing it from his face and revealing his matching goatee. "Just taking a little breather."

"Okay," I hollered back, "but y'all really need to put a dive flag out. It's Friday and the boat traffic will be picking up in this area."

"We're new at this," the smaller diver said in a clearly feminine voice. Her hair was an unnatural yellow-blonde with an even more unnatural blue strip stringing down on one side of her face. "Thanks for the reminder. We'll do that, and be more careful."

"We'll leave you to it, then," I called back. "Stay safe." I puttered away from the divers and then pressed down on the throttle.

"Wonder what they were doing?" Millie shouted above the wind and engine noise.

"A lot of people dive Smith Lake," I called back. "Whole towns were flooded when this lake was made. Some divers have actually brought up merchandise found in old storefronts down there. I guess every little thing wasn't cleared out of some places."

"Dead bodies have been found here too," Millie said, standing and moving beside me. "I saw a news segment not too long ago about a car some divers found when the highway department was getting ready to make some bridge repairs. The driver was still in it, and had been missing since the '70s. Creepy."

"I remember that too," I replied. "And you know Larry's niece's husband Adam? He and his family have a towing service. Just a couple weeks ago, he was called out to use his wrecker to pull a Maserati out of the water."

"Was anyone inside?" Millie asked, shuddering.

"Nope. It seems the owner had reported it stolen. I don't think that will turn out to be the case. Who steals a Maserati just to sink it? No, I think it'll turn out to be insurance fraud—too much car and not enough money."

Millie went back to her seat and we rode the rest of the way to the marina in silence, admiring the view and enjoying the whole experience. As soon as the boat slips came into view, I started slowing, knowing the no-wake buoy was right around the corner.

"Throw the rope over that cleat," I instructed Millie as I edged the boat against the floating dock.

After I secured the back of the boat with another rope, we stepped onto the wooden walkway. "Look up there," I said, pointing to a large outcropping of rock high above the shoreline. "That's why this place is called Rock Ledge."

"Picturesque. I think I feel a painting coming on." Millie

slipped her phone from a pocket in her cover-up and snapped a few photos.

"I feel a fish feeding coming on," I said, stepping through the doorway of the tiny store. "Grab us each a baby bottle and I'll buy the crackers."

Seconds later, we were seated on the edge of the dock with our legs dangling in the clear blue-green water. We unscrewed the tops from our baby bottles and crammed the bottles full of crackers. We then pushed the bottles underwater so they would fill with water before we replaced the tops.

"How do the fish suck the crackers out of such a tiny hole?" Millie asked.

"Look again," I said. "They've cut an X in the end of the nipple. They won't have a problem getting all the crackers."

"Here comes one!" Millie squealed excitedly, as a 20- or 30-pound carp rose to inspect us. Lowering her upside down baby bottle into the water, Millie held tightly as the big fish set in to drain the bottle. But before that could happen, he was jostled out of position by an even bigger fish.

"Time for the real test of nerves," I said, lifting one foot and sticking a cracker between my big and second toe. "Let's see you feed one this way." By the time my foot was back in the water, a mammoth carp had latched onto my toes, slurping up the entire cracker before it had time to disintegrate in the water.

"No way!" Millie said. "I don't want one of those things to bite me!"

"They don't bite," I assured her. "No teeth. Just try it. It tickles, that's all."

By the time we'd let the carp polish off an entire sleeve of crackers, we were laughing hysterically and drawing a crowd of newcomers. "I think it's time we get out of the way and let these other folks have some carp time," I said. "My stomach tells me it's time to feed ourselves."

4

After a short ride on the main body of the lake, I pulled the boat into Simmons Slough, a remote inlet in another section of the Bankhead Forest where the tall rock bluffs had become a popular spot for jumping and diving. With nothing but 50 feet of water below them, it was as safe as it gets for anyone brave enough to climb up there.

"Have you been up on those bluffs?" Millie asked.

"Yes," I admitted, "but it was on a dare, and I only jumped once. I couldn't count how many times Larry's dove off there. Not me."

"Me either," Millie said. "Still, I bet there's a pretty view from up there."

"The only view I'm interested in right now is a look at my tomato sandwich," I said. We were munching away in no time.

Stuffing the now empty containers into the cooler, I fished out our one remaining treat—we'd eaten the grapes on the way to the marina. "Ready for a brownie?" I asked, holding one aloft temptingly.

"Book and brownie," Millie said. "Now that's a winning combination."

Spreading our towels on the front deck, we polished off the brownies while enjoying a little rest and reading time. "If you aren't going to take a nap," I said, "I'm going to see if I can."

"You go right ahead," Millie said, "Hercule and I will be watching over you."

"Thanks," I said. "It's too deep to anchor here, and I don't want to float into the rocks and risk damaging the pontoon. Move us out if we float in too close to the bank. The paddles are under the bench, or you can start the motor if you need to."

"Will do," Millie said. "I know you didn't get as much sleep as I did last night."

Rolling onto my stomach and wadding up my cover-up as a pillow, I was instantly unconscious. And almost as quickly awake again.

"Where was their boat?" Millie asked, rousing me out of oblivion.

"Huh? What?" I mumbled.

"The divers. Where was their boat?" Millie repeated.

"Maybe they didn't have one. Maybe they hiked in through the Bankhead and walked to the water," I said, my voice muffled by half my face being buried in my makeshift pillow.

"I guess that's possible," Millie agreed, "but that'd be an awfully long way to lug all that heavy equipment. And it sure would limit where they'd be able to dive. I mean, wouldn't they want a boat where they could move around to other places?"

"They said they were new divers," I reminded her. "Maybe they don't own a boat. Maybe they just wanted to try out their gear. Maybe I can get my nap now if you're all out of questions."

"Sorry," Millie said, not sounding the least bit apologetic. "Carry on. I'll go back to my book now."

When I awoke the next time, the sun had moved enough for the bluffs to cast a welcome shadow over the pontoon. "Goodness!" I said. "How long did I sleep? Why didn't you wake me?"

"Almost two hours," Millie answered. "And I may have unintentionally nodded off for a little bit myself."

"Well, at least we're still not too close to the bank," I said. "How about a swim? Here or back at Jane's?"

"Let's go back to Jane's," Millie said. We might even do a little fishing tonight if you want to."

"I'm not comfortable taking a boat out at night," I said.

"Not in the boat," Millie explained. "Off the swim pier. That might be fun."

"What are we going to fish with?" I asked.

"There are tons of fishing equipment in the laundry room, and I brought a pack of weenies I'm willing to sacrifice as catfish bait,"

Millie answered.

"That'll work," I said. I hoisted myself off the floor of the deck and slid into the driver's seat. "Make sure we have everything locked down so nothing can blow away," I reminded her.

We sped by a number of houses and arrived back at the stretch of Bankhead where we'd seen the divers. "No one there now," I said. "Let's take the left fork and see if we see them again. Maybe they moved to a different location."

We turned away from the direction of Jane's and rounded a bend that led farther into the forest. Here, the land ran straight into the water, terracing off into shallow and then deeper shelves of pink and yellow sandstone. There were no signs of divers or a boat.

Swinging around to head back toward Jane's, we again reached the spot where we'd seen the divers. "Look there!" Millie pointed. "What are those marks?" She indicated some scrapes along the sandstone only a few feet above the water line.

"Maybe from the divers' tanks?" I suggested. "But I can't help but wonder how they got here. I don't know of any roads through this part of the woods, unless there's some sort of fire lane. Blazing a trail through all that would risk serious damage, even to a Jeep or any other four-wheel drive."

"Sure seems like a lot of trouble to go through for beginner divers," Millie said.

And I agreed. "But it was a couple. Maybe they've got a camping permit and are spending a few days in the Bankhead. A budget-friendly way to have some alone time."

"Certainly a possibility," Millie said. "Let's have that swim now, and then I'll throw some chicken breasts on the grill. I put them in marinade before we left this morning."

"Mmmm," I said. "Perfect."

It was dusky dark by the time we finished our chicken, baked potatoes, and salads. After clearing everything from the porch, we made quick work of kitchen clean-up. Then, books in hand, we claimed opposite ends of the sofa and went back to our reading.

When I saw the hands of the mantel clock creeping toward 9:00 p.m., I picked up the remote. "Okay if I turn on the news?" I asked.

"Sure," Millie answered. "Let's see what's going on beyond our little paradise."

"Well, there seems to be trouble in paradise," I said. "I called Larry when we first came back in, and he said they'll probably be telling about a carjacking that happened up this way this morning."

"Good grief!" Millie said. "The lake is supposed to be peaceful and relaxing!"

"Wait," I interrupted. "Looks like this is the story."

A stern-faced Steve Cofer stared into the camera. The words

"Special Report" were emblazoned across the backdrop behind him. At six foot six, Steve towered over everyone else at the station and his mahogany skin made his perfect white teeth gleam like a toothpaste commercial.

"Good evening," he said. "You're watching the WEEE News at Nine. Is anyone safe these days? It would seem not, when the pastor of a church gets carjacked right in the church's parking lot. Reporter Melanie Posten is with us live from Winston County at Simmons Chapel Community Church. Melanie, what can you tell us?"

The studio vanished and the parking lot and sign for the Simmons Chapel Community Church appeared, with Melanie Posten holding a microphone and standing next to a slender, middle-aged white guy wearing a Crimson Tide t-shirt and blue jeans. A hazy image of a white wooden church appeared in the background. A banner at the bottom of the screen identified the man as Rev. Victor Pratt.

"Reverend Pratt," Melanie began, her blonde-tipped pixie cut causing my jaw to drop.

I paused Melanie in mid-sentence and turned to Millie. "When Melanie told me to look for a change tonight, I didn't expect anything so drastic. Isn't she fabulous?"

"She looks really sharp, but her up do was adorable too," Millie responded. "And look at that cute, cute dress. Let's face it. She'd look great even if she shaved her head."

"When I saw her at the station yesterday …" I began. "Wow,

with all that's happened, that seems like a century ago. Anyhow, she said she had a hair appointment and was ready for a change. She sure made one." I grabbed my phone and sent a quick text telling the popular reporter, "Love the new do." Then I hit the play button and Melanie continued.

"Can you describe what happened here this morning?" Melanie held the microphone toward the obviously uncomfortable man.

"I pastor this church," he said, motioning toward the building with one hand, "and I pretty much have a routine way of doing things. I come in around 8:00 a.m. and work on my sermon, check the messages on the church phone, and see who might need help or prayer or just a visit."

"And that's your weekday routine?" Melanie asked, moving the microphone back to herself and then back to Reverend Pratt.

"Except on Wednesday mornings …" the Reverend began.

Melanie swiftly cut in. "But yesterday morning, Thursday, wasn't so routine, was it?" she asked. "Describe what happened when you got here."

"I'd just parked my truck and got out to go inside the church when two fellas came out from the side of the building. "The minute I laid eyes on them, I knew they were up to no good. The biggest one said, 'We're gonna need those keys, preacher.'"

"Did they threaten you?" Melanie questioned.

"After he told me he wanted my keys, he said, 'And as long as you hand 'em over, we won't hurt you.' The smaller one didn't say anything, but I didn't hesitate to give 'em my keys. No truck is worth getting killed over," Reverend Pratt added, shaking his head. "They got in and drove off."

"Did you recognize either of them?" Melanie continued.

"They were both wearing ski masks," Reverend Pratt responded. "You know, the kind that goes over your head and only has holes for your eyes and mouth. But I could see enough skin to tell they were white. And I'd say the bigger one would go about six foot and 200 pounds. Jeans and a long-sleeved chambray shirt. The other fella was a good bit shorter and was wearing one of those long canvas coats like you see movie cowboys in sometimes. Dusters, I think they're called."

"Was anything of value inside the vehicle?" Melanie asked, again doing the flip-flop with the microphone.

"No," said the Reverend. "I'd already taken my briefcase out, and my Bible was in it. Wouldn't have wanted to lose that, but those two sure could benefit from the Good Book, if they'd take the time to read it."

"Thank you for talking with us," Melanie said. "And we're so sorry for what you've experienced." Turning to the audience, she added, "Reverend Pratt has provided us with a photo of his truck and you see it now on your screen. If you see this truck or have any information that could help police find the men who committed this crime, you're urged to call the Winston County Sheriff's Department at the number on your screen. The truck is a black 1997 Chevrolet Silverado 4-wheel drive, tag number ..."

"That poor man," Millie said. "I know he was terrified."

"And I'm guessing he only had liability insurance since the truck was that old. He probably won't be getting reimbursed for it, but thank the Lord he wasn't hurt. It could have been much worse."

"That's for sure," Millie concurred.

When Melanie's segment ended, we were bombarded with commercials before the news came back on. I was surprised to see Melanie still on camera. Looks like she was stealing all the limelight tonight.

"Melanie," Steve's voice said from the news desk, "I understand you also have an update on the body found in Lewis Smith Lake yesterday."

"That's right, Steve," Melanie answered, pitch blackness behind her. Apparently she'd only had time to move Reverend Pratt out of the shot and angle herself so the church wouldn't be on camera.

"The identity of the body discovered yesterday in a remote part of Lewis Smith Lake has now been released. The victim's name is Bobby Joe Benson, age 34. Mr. Benson was a resident of Dovertown, a small mining community about twenty miles southwest of Fall Creek."

The screen split between Melanie's remote shot and the newsroom, where Steve asked the next question: "Melanie, when you say 'victim,' are you saying foul play was involved?"

"Not at this point, Steve," she responded. "Winston County's coroner, Dr. Lizzie Okada, has refused to make any speculations.

She says we'll have to wait until she completes the autopsy. Now back to you in the studio."

We watched the rest of the news in silence. As I switched off the TV, Millie drummed her fingers against her book. "Why does the name Simmons sound so familiar?" Millie asked.

"We were in Simmons Slough when we had our lunch today. Simmons Chapel is probably no more than two miles from there, as the crow flies."

"How creepy is that!" Millie shuddered.

"You still want to go fishing tonight?" I asked her, "or are you scared like I was last night?"

"You," Millie said, "were scared of a nonexistent prowler. I, on the other hand, have seen live on TV that there are two scary men running around this area somewhere."

"Or they're umpteen miles from here by now, in all probability," I countered. "I'd bet everybody around Simmons Chapel knows what that preacher drives. It's a small community. I wouldn't stick around here driving something so many people would recognize."

"Point taken," Millie conceded. "Let's put on some long pants and gather up some fishing gear."

"And the bug repellent," I added. "We'll be mosquito bait without it."

My phone did its staccato notes for a text and I pulled it from my pocket and saw "TY, sweetie" and a smiley emoji blowing a kiss. It was Melanie acknowledging my message about her hairdo.

I reeled up the first catfish and landed its flopping body on the swim pier. "Hand me those grippers," I said, pointing to an orange plastic contraption that would help me hold the fish still while I got the hook out.

"Be careful," Millie warned, as she watched me using one hand to hold the fish in the gripper while I worked at the hook with the other.

"You want to keep these?" I asked. "I'll take them off the hook, but count me out when it comes to cleaning them."

"Don't you remember how Uncle Ellis would nail their heads to a board and then cut around the head and use pliers ..."

"Stop right there," I interrupted. "I remember Daddy's method in all too vivid detail. And if you will recall, I always ran for the hills whenever he started. I like my fish like I like my beef and pork and chicken: already dead and neatly packaged or prepared before I have to look at it."

"In that case, it's a catch-and-release night," Millie declared, "because I'm sure not cleaning them. Now I wish Larry or Bill were here. Neither one of them would mind doing it."

"We can always drive over to Seafood King," I suggested.

"And tomorrow night's their seafood buffet!" Millie suddenly remembered. "And there's always catfish too."

"I know where we're having dinner tomorrow night," I said.

Larry wasn't a seafood person. He could eat his weight in almost any kind of fish, but he was no fan of, as he was known to say, "anything that crawled, walked, wiggled, flew, or otherwise came out of the water without fins and gills."

Not that I didn't appreciate Millie's company anyway, but she came in especially handy when there was seafood around. Down at the beautiful white sand beaches of Gulf Shores, Alabama, it was so nice to have her or my writer friend Sammie around to split the humongous seafood platter at Lulu's, a popular spot on the Intracoastal Waterway owned by the restaurant's namesake, who happens to be the sister of singer/songwriter Jimmy Buffett. One normal human could never finish off one of those platters singlehandedly.

I rebaited and dropped my line back into the water, letting out a good 20 feet of line to get my bait down to the same depth where I'd caught the first fish. Millie was reeling up her first catch before I even finished letting out my line.

After releasing her fish, Millie rinsed her hands, wiped them on one of the rags we'd brought from the laundry room, and began to flail her arms back and forth all around her head. "Can we turn the light off?" she asked. "These bugs are driving me buggy." As she spoke, she sprayed a fog of insect repellent all around her.

"Sure," I said. "I dropped a flashlight in the tote with all that other stuff I brought down. We can turn it on when we need to take a hook out."

We fished in silence for an hour or so, or rather, attempted to.

"I guess ..." I began, but an enormous splash far out to our right startled me into silence.

"What was that?" Millie asked quietly and nervously. "Sounded as big as an elephant."

But before I could explain how sound traveled and amplified over water, we distinctly heard human voices. "Shhh," I whispered. "Listen."

Many's the time Larry and I had sat out in our boat and heard entire conversations coming from porches, piers, and even open windows as we trolled along the lake or river. The voices we were hearing had to be pretty far away because we could only hear bits and pieces as the wind wafted a word or two in our direction.

"Tonight," a low male voice said. Everything else was garbled rumbling.

"T.J.," another voice said. Or was it B.J.? I couldn't be certain.

"Whoever it is," Millie whispered, "they don't know anybody else is out here. I say we give them their privacy and go inside. I don't like this at all."

I totally agreed with her, but I couldn't resist getting a barb in. "Is this your way of telling me you're scared?" I whispered back.

"Yes, and double yes," she answered. "Now let's get this stuff together and get behind locked doors."

We made it to the house with no problems, did a double-check on all the doors and windows, and then took our showers. And yes, I'm not ashamed to say I slept in Millie's room again. After all, as scared as she was, I figured she could use the company.

Saturday morning, over breakfast on the porch, Millie and I discussed the voices from the previous night. "You know," I said, "we read too many mysteries. We turn everything into one. Those voices we heard last night were probably just some guys out fishing or on the pier of that house around the bend."

"You're probably right," Millie conceded, "but they sure sounded close."

"That's the water. It carries sound like a megaphone."

"And what about that enormous splash?" Millie asked. "What could that have been?"

I had to laugh this time. "Not another body, that's for certain. I was so keyed up last night after hearing those voices that I didn't use an ounce of logic. Smith Lake is known for big fish: largemouth bass, striped bass, carp, and even gars as big as barracudas. Any of those jumping could have made that loud a noise."

"Whew! That's a relief to know," Millie said. "I figured it was criminals tossing in another body." We both laughed and agreed that our imaginations had been working overtime.

"It's early—only 8:15. Let's get dressed and hit some yard sales before all the good stuff is gone," I suggested. "Then we can check out some thrift stores and consignment shops later in the day."

"Let's make a whole day of it," Millie said. "And since we're going into Fall Creek to Seafood King, we can see what shops are around town."

"An excellent idea," I said, grinning. "It's so nice to have a shopping buddy who appreciates a bargain as much as I do."

As Millie padded off toward her bedroom, she called back, "Don't forget your occasions list. I'm putting mine in my jeans pocket."

The occasions list is a money-saver I came up with years ago. It's a plain ol' sheet of paper with the names of everyone I plan to buy a gift for all year long written down the left column. Out beside each name are notes about their sizes, birthdays, wedding dates, etc. And at the bottom of the page, I even include headings for miscellaneous bridal teas, baby teas, and graduations. Then, with my occasions list handy, I keep an eye out for the perfect bargain for all these occasions and note each purchase beside the appropriate column.

Since I've talked, written, and done TV segments about it, the occasions list has become a must-have for many of my Bargainomics fans. I couldn't begin to count the number of people who, after starting their own occasions lists, have contacted me to tell me they were spending 75 percent less and giving better gifts to boot. I love knowing my tips are helping others.

Before I could head inside to get dressed, my phone chirped and I saw the caller was Kiki Roberts. Millie and I had met Kiki at Whiter Than Snow, a free laundry service and outreach of Chalybeate Springs Community Church.

With a trailer park full of immigrants and other low-income families not far from the church, the free laundry was truly a godsend. We also used the facility for afterschool tutoring, ESL (English as a Second Language) classes, and Bible studies. Millie and I volunteered as teachers, and Larry and Bill kept the washers and dryers in working order.

Since moving to Chalybeate Springs, Kiki had gotten her GED, completed a cosmetology course at Bevill State Community College, and gone to work at Cheveux, a classy salon owned by her cousin Walter's wife, Diamond Purifoy. Until Kiki joined the stylists at Cheveux, Millie and I had never met Diamond, but we had become acquainted with Walter, an officer with the Birmingham Police Department, when he'd accompanied our friend Detective Metz on a stakeout that had nearly gotten both of them killed and hadn't been a particularly fun occasion for me and Millie.

"Hey, Kiki," I said, punching the speaker button on my phone as I swallowed the last sip of my iced tea. "What's going on?"

"I'm up to my eyeballs in customers," Kiki replied, clearly

pleased to have built up such a sizable clientele. "I wanted to take a minute to check with you and see if it's all right if we throw a little surprise party for Lisa and Kenny after class next Friday."

"Refresh my memory, girl," I responded. "What's the occasion?" Lisa Noles was another friend we'd met through Whiter Than Snow. She and Kiki had completed their cosmetology courses together and Lisa was coming up on her second drug-free year since joining N.A. (Narcotics Anonymous), an occasion certainly worth celebrating. Kenny Mankiller was yet another member of our Whiter Than Snow family, but I couldn't think of any sort of milestone coming up in his life.

"Kenny was just made foreman at Dartwell Farms," Kiki announced, pride for her fellow Bible student and friend adding lilt to her voice. "And," she continued, "Kenny told me he thought the party would be the perfect time to pop the question to Lisa."

"What!" I yelped, lifting the phone closer to my mouth. "I didn't even know they were dating."

Kiki cackled over my surprise. "Naw, girlfriend. I was just messin' with you. I just think they both could use some special recognition."

"Well, I agree. Sounds like a great idea all the way 'round," I answered. "You really had me going for a minute there," I chided. "I may not be the most observant person on the planet, but I'd have surely known if they'd already been dating."

"You ain't missed a thing, honey-lamb," Kiki promised. "If you'll help pass the word, Diamond said she'd help me make the cake. And if a few others will pitch in on some finger foods and drinks, we'll be good to go."

"That'll work," I said. "Millie's with me, so I'll let her know and she can help contact everybody else."

"Thank you, hon," Kiki responded. "Gotta run. See you Friday."

Dashing into the house, I stuck my empty glass in the fridge and hurriedly threw on clothes and a little bit of makeup. Then, occasions lists at the ready, Millie and I hit the road. We'd barely covered two miles when we saw a hand-printed yard sale sign pointing out a long gravel drive. When we cleared the wooded access road, a massive two-story log house stood before us, its wraparound porch lined with furniture and other yard sale goodies. More items were on tables underneath a blue vinyl canopy. Three other vehicles were already ahead of us, one a battered van I immediately recognized.

"Martha Jones," I said to Millie. "She has a booth at the flea market. If she's here, we better hurry. She'll buy anything she can make a few dollars on."

"If it'll fit in her van, you mean," Millie said. "Look at all that furniture."

"Oh, no," I replied. "If she buys more than the van will hold, she'll call her husband and he'll bring his pickup to get the rest of it. So we better hurry," I added, already bailing from the car. Millie was barely a step behind me. While she headed for the canopy, I went for the porch.

"Good morning," a feminine voice greeted me. A dark-haired woman in her late 20s or early 30s was seated in an overstuffed chair that matched the sofa beside it.

"Good morning," I said. "Looks like you're cleaning house."

"Top to bottom," she said. "And I'm negotiable on just about everything. I need to get this place cleared out."

"Are you selling?" I asked. I hadn't noticed a sale sign on the roadway.

"Actually, we just bought this place," she explained. "It was an estate sale—the owner had passed away—and we bought it lock, stock, and barrel. We're only keeping a handful of things. The rest, we've piled out here, hoping to sell most of it."

"Well, toward the end of the day, you can expect a return visit from that gray-haired lady over there," I said, pointing toward Martha, who was digging through a cardboard box of linens. "She'll make you an offer on the whole shebang, whatever's left. She resells at a flea market not far from where I live."

And then it came. "You look so familiar," the lady said. "I'm Kelli Newell," she said. "And you are?"

"Judy Bates," I offered, extending my hand to shake hers. "Nice to meet you, Kelli."

"Wait a minute," Kelli said, a bit of excitement mounting in her voice. "You're not that lady from TV, are you? That, uh, wait a minute … Bargainomics Lady! That's it. You're not her, are you?"

"'Fraid I am," I laughed. "My cousin," I said, pointing to

Millie, "and I are staying at a friend's lake house this week."

"Omigosh," Kelli said. "My mama went to grammar school with you! Hang on a sec." She hopped up, yanked open the screen door, and hollered, "Mama, you're not gonna believe who's here! Come out here!"

A minute or so later, out walked a short, sandy-haired lady whom I immediately recognized. "Faye Gilliam!" I squealed. "How wonderful to see you!"

Grabbing me in a hug, Faye responded, "I've been a Busby ever since I got out of high school. Talk about a small world! It's so good to see you in person. I've told Kelli we went to school together. Even told her about our adventure climbing that bluff on the side of Highway 78."

"If my mother were still living, she'd skin me alive today if she found out about that," I laughed. Faye and I had had some adventures together.

Kelli interrupted our reunion. "Can we get a picture together? I can't believe I have a TV celebrity at my yard sale!"

"Sure," I said, thinking that I didn't consider five minutes a week exactly qualified me for celebrity status. But Kelli was thrilled, and who was I to burst her bubble?

"Millie," I called. "Would you come over here and take a photo for us, please?"

Millie looked up, rolled her eyes, and smiled sarcastically. "Certainly," she said. I knew I was in for a ribbing when we got back in the car.

"Just touch that little circle right there," Kelli instructed Millie as she handed over her cell phone. I stepped between Kelli and Faye, and Millie snapped the pic and returned the phone to Kelli, who immediately began uploading our photo to Facebook. "My friends are going to be so jealous that I got to meet you in person!" Kelli beamed.

Millie, who, by then, was standing behind Kelli and Faye, stuck one finger into her open mouth and made a gagging motion. One of her greatest pleasures in life is giving me a hard time about the people who treat me like a movie star.

The one I'll never live down is the day Millie and I were walking back to her car in the parking lot of a strip mall. Suddenly we heard a lady's voice calling, "Yoo-hoo! Bargainomics Lady! C'mere!" Looking around, I spotted a battered pickup truck with a blonde lady hanging out the window, a half-burned cigarette between the fingers of her waving hand.

Millie arched an eyebrow and continued toward her car. "You're going over there with me," I hissed.

"I can't believe this!" the 40-ish woman in the truck kept saying. "The Bargainomics Lady right here in person! I'm sorry for all that hollerin'," she said, "but I've got my grandbaby with me and I didn't want to leave him in here by hisself while I chased after you." She nodded toward the sleeping infant sprawled on the seat beside her.

"What an angel," I said, leaning through a cloud of cigarette smoke to admire the little cotton-top.

"Yeah, he's a keeper," the woman said, smiling and revealing an incomplete set of discolored teeth. Can I get a pitcher with you?" she continued, digging around the cluttered interior of the pickup. "Oh, no," she moaned. "Here you are and I ain't even got my phone with me. Will you take one and send it to me?"

"I'm so sorry," I insincerely told her, "but I don't have my phone with me." That last part was true. It was in Millie's car.

"Well, can I at least get your autograph?" she pleaded. "Hang on just a second." She began sorting through the trash in the floorboard, finally coming up with a grimy bag from Whataburger, complete with the ground-in imprint of what looked to be a work boot sole.

"Here," she said, tearing off a portion of the sack. "The inside's clean. Make sure you write on that side. Make it to Regina," she said. "R-e-g-i-n-a."

She handed me a well-chewed pencil and I added her name to my usual note: "Happy bargain hunting, Regina!" and signed it "Judy, the Bargainomics Lady."

"Thank you so much!" she beamed, a thin line of smoke curling up from her cigarette.

"You're very welcome," I said. "And it was nice to meet you," I said, feeling guilty for my second stretch of the truth that day.

Millie fluttered a few fingers in a farewell wave and we set out across the parking lot for Millie's car. As soon as we were out of earshot, Millie said, "And you didn't even introduce me," an evil grin spreading across her face.

"Oh, hush!" I snapped as Millie slid behind the wheel. "Just pass me the hand sanitizer." I cleaned my hands, hoping the nastiness from my autograph paper hadn't already invaded my body.

"This was one for the record books," Millie said, shaking her head. "Remember that man and woman in the motor home?"

"Don't go there," I warned. That was yet another unpleasant fan experience.

"And that poor baby," Millie said. "He had to be either deaf or unconscious."

"I suspect Regina and her crew do a lot of hollering," I said. "He's probably used to loud noises."

"Bless his sweet little heart," Millie added. "And breathing all that smoke too. There oughta be a law against it."

"In some states, there is," I said, "but Alabama's not one of them. A bill was introduced to ban smoking in a car when a child is present, but it passed in the House and got voted down in the Senate. Hopefully it'll be reintroduced one of these days."

After chatting with Martha and a couple other shoppers who had recognized me from television, Faye and I hugged again and promised to stay in touch. Then Millie and I headed to the car, each with our own newfound treasure. Millie had some old keys I knew she'd use in some sort of artwork. I found a really cute wooden sign, "Life at the lake is better," and bought it to leave as a gift for Jane. I knew she'd love it.

Back out on the blacktop, we kept our eyes peeled for more

yard sale signs. We put the windows down and leisurely cruised past woods and pastureland, eventually spotting another sign, this time directing us to "Yard Sale Ahead: 1 mile."

"Deer!" Millie suddenly screeched, as a round-bellied doe bounded into the road. Slamming on my brakes, we came to a halt and waited. Where there's one, there are usually more. Sure enough, seconds later, two more does trotted out. I waited a few additional seconds in case of stragglers, and then we were on our way.

"Ladies," Millie shouted out the window at the departing deer, "you need to be more careful, especially in your condition." All three were obviously carrying fawns that would likely be born within the next few weeks.

"I thought deer had their babies earlier in the summer," Millie commented.

"I'd asked Larry about that before," I said, "and he told me that Alabama deer are sometimes as late as February breeding, which means the babies aren't born until late summer or even early fall."

"Learn something new every day," Millie responded.

We'd been the sole car on the road thus far, but as I glanced in the rearview mirror, I noticed a dark vehicle coming up from behind. I sped up a bit since I'd been barely crawling, but the dark blob was still gaining. A third check of the mirror and I could make out the front end of a Chevy pickup.

"I'm going five miles over the speed limit now," I said, as if the driver could hear me. "If you want to go faster, you'll just have to pass." Apparently he did hear me because the black pickup blew by my Hyundai like we were standing still.

"Hey!" I said, addressing Millie this time. "That looks like the truck that was stolen from that preacher over in Simmons Chapel!"

"Did you get the license number?" Millie asked.

"Why, yes," I responded, "and the VIN number too."

"I can do without your sarcasm," Millie said. "Maybe it was one of your fans and they've put up a roadblock ahead so you'll have to stop and meet him. He might even have a sandwich wrapper you can sign."

"You are so hilarious," I returned. "Ha, ha. Here is me laughing. That guy went by so fast I barely had time to blink. All I can say for sure is I didn't see anyone in the truck besides the driver."

"Should we call the police?" Millie asked.

"And tell them what?" I responded. "That a black Chevy truck just passed us? How many of those do you think are around these parts? If we see it again, we'll try to get a closer look. Then we can pull up the news report online and compare the tag numbers."

"Okay," Millie agreed. "Turn there," she added, indicating a drive on the opposite side of the road. "That's the yard sale." The sale was mostly clothes, none of which were either of our sizes, but Millie lucked out finding a huge framed print for only five dollars.

"That is one ugly picture," I said, curling my lip as Millie loaded her find into the Hyundai.

"You know I didn't buy it for the print," Millie responded. "You're the one who introduced me to buying for the value of the frame. A frame like this is worth at least a hundred dollars."

"Probably more than that," I said. "That's mahogany and gold gilt. You done big, cuz."

"Thank you," she said. "I have learned from the master." She bowed her head in my direction.

"Cute," I retorted. "I wonder if Seafood King does lunch. I'm starving."

"I'm pretty hungry myself. You always have snacks in the car," she said, reaching for a zippered lunch bag. "Want to munch on some of those?"

"No, I'll be dead if I don't get a real meal soon," I whined. "Shopping is hard work."

The clock on the wall ahead of us showed 11:55 as we walked through the front door of Seafood King in Fall Creek. The place was already busy and there was a crowd around the buffet table, or "trough," as Millie and I had come to call them.

A cheerful guy in a red polo shirt with a Seafood King logo— a happy-faced fish standing on his tail with one fin wrapped around an equally happy shrimp and the other around a surprisingly cheerful crab—welcomed us, menus in hand. "Will you two lovely ladies be dining in?" he asked. Then turning to me, he asked, "I've seen you here before, haven't I?"

"Yes, we'll be dining in and, yes, you've probably seen me here," I responded, "although it's been a while."

"I thought I recognized you," he said. Millie stared down at the floor and I had no doubt she was rolling her eyes again.

"Table or booth?" he asked.

"Booth," I answered. "But first, may we take a look at the buffet, please?"

"Certainly," he answered. "My name is Ollie. Take all the time you need. But I should tell you the seafood selection is much larger after 5:00 p.m."

If the selection was any bigger at night, we didn't need to go near it. There was already enough there to make our taste buds dance with joy.

Ollie directed us to a booth and took our drink orders before we scurried to hit the trough. I found a small cup and ladled in a luscious-smelling seafood chowder, snagged a few packs of saltines, and went back to our table. Millie followed suit, but chose a shrimp bisque instead.

"Mmmm," Millie mumbled, savoring her first taste of the bisque. "You've gotta try this." I reached a spoon across to dip up a sample.

"I meant go get some of your own and try it," she said, pulling the cup out of my reach.

Millie and I grew up tasting and sharing each other's food.

After her bout with cancer, though, she had justifiably become a bit of a germophobe. Can't say that I blamed her, either.

I trotted back to the trough and ladled up a tiny sample of the shrimp bisque. Millie was right. It was marvelous. But so were the crab cakes—not too bready, which is an absolute no-no in my book. We both overindulged in boiled shrimp with an outstanding house-made cocktail sauce. And the catfish that had started us thinking about Seafood King in the first place? They had it fried, grilled, and blackened.

"No oysters?" Millie asked.

"They're not in season," I reminded her, "unless there's an R in the month. August. No R, no oysters. Unless they've been frozen."

"Why's that?" Millie asked.

"I don't know," I answered. "Because that's what Mother always told me."

"Well, if Aunt Sybil said it, that's good enough for me," Millie responded.

We both made the decision to skip the corn-on-the-cob and baked potatoes. "Let's stick with salad and a few hushpuppies," Millie suggested. "That way, we can tank up on catfish and seafood."

"Good idea." I placed my plateful of shrimp peelings at the edge of the table, slid from the booth, and answered one more call to the trough before calling it quits.

We waddled out of Seafood King declaring we wouldn't eat

again for three days. That lasted until we saw the sign for DQ and decided we could pick up Blizzards and call them supper that evening.

"I think if we go around back," I said, "there's a road that cuts over toward Divine Consigns. Okay if we make it our first stop?"

"Sure," Millie said.

The parking lot had been pretty full, but the back of the restaurant had quite a few vehicles too. I figured it took a lot of employees to serve a spread like we'd just feasted on.

At the dumpster, I hit the brakes. "Isn't that the same truck that passed us while ago?" I asked. A black Chevy pickup was wedged between the dumpster and the concrete retaining wall behind it.

"Sure looks like it," Millie said. "Sit tight while I take a pic of the tag."

"Be careful," I warned. "I can't tell if anyone's in it or not."

As Millie neared the dumpster, a light-haired guy in a chef's apron came out a screen door at the back of the restaurant. Spotting me in my car and my passenger door standing open, his eyes swung around to Millie. "Everything all right, ladies?" he asked politely.

"Uh, yeah," I said. "She thought she saw a kitten over there by the dumpster. We didn't want to leave the little guy to fend for itself."

"There's always cats around here, ma'am," the cook responded.

Millie reached the back of the truck and pulled out her phone. A split second later, the truck engine roared to life and I stifled a scream. Thankfully, the driver zoomed forward, speeding into the alleyway and leaving a cloud of dust and fumes behind him.

"Who the ..." Still sharing his opinion as to the truck driver's lineage, the cook sprinted toward Millie. "You okay, ma'am? Good thing that guy didn't throw it in reverse."

"S-sure was," Millie stammered, clearly a bit shaken. "But I'm f-fine."

"Did you find the kitten?" he asked.

Frantically waving behind his back, I leaned toward the passenger window and called, "I think it was just a mouse," I said, hoping she'd pick up on my phony explanation.

And she did. "You're probably right," she answered, walking back toward the car.

"Wouldn't surprise me none," the cook said. "I've seen gophers out here that could swallow a house cat." Dropping into a rusty metal folding chair beside the screen door, the cook pulled out his cell phone and punched in a number. "You ladies be careful and have a good evening." With that, he directed his attention to his phone call, and Millie and I made our departure.

"Did you get the tag number? That was so dangerous!" I chided. "We're not taking any more crazy chances."

"Agreed," Millie said. "But I got us a perfect image of that tag. If it's the same one reported on the news last night, we'll call the police."

71

"And while we're calling," I added, "we better call on the Lord to forgive us for all these fibs we've been telling."

"But for a good cause," Millie said, defensively.

"Maybe so," I agreed, "but I still plan to 'have a little talk with Jesus' before I go to bed tonight."

At Divine Consigns, I had a chance to practice my parallel parking. After only three attempts, I succeeded.

"You'd think you were parking a Mack truck," Millie laughed.

"Hey, how often do you have to parallel park?" I asked. "This is not a skill I get much practice at."

"Hang on a sec," Millie said, as I reached for the door handle. "Let's check out that tag number first."

"Okey-doke," I said, as Millie began fiddling with her phone.

"Wait a minute," she said. "Look it up on your phone. I'll keep mine on the photo."

Hitting WEEE's website, I scrolled to the info about the carjacking. "Here it is: AJC5172," I read.

"Omigosh," Millie said, inhaling sharply. "That's it. That's the truck that was stolen."

"The sheriff's department is a block down. Let's walk over there and report it in person," I suggested.

We climbed a short set of steps and entered the building. A deputy stood guard at a metal detector. "Good afternoon, ladies,"

he said as Millie plopped her purse on the conveyer belt.

"If there's a phone in there, ma'am, you need to remove it and place it in the dish, please," he instructed.

"Oh, sorry," Millie said. "This is my first time to go to jail." Red-faced, Millie added, "I don't mean *to* jail. I mean this is my first time to be *in* jail. Oh …"

"I think he understands what you mean, Millie," I interrupted her. I handed her a white plastic bowl for her cell phone.

I dropped my phone, keys, and coin purse into another bowl and waited for my turn to pass through the detector. I rarely carried a purse anymore. I'd bought a coin purse with an I.D. window for my driver's license, plus room for my debit card, a little cash, and a mini lip gloss. I keep it clipped to my belt loop or waistband and hidden neatly under my shirt. My phone goes in my pants pocket. This way, my hands are free and, unlike a certain someone carrying a two-ton satchel, I'm not an outstanding target for a mugger.

Once we cleared the screening process, we were directed to a pair of glass doors, behind which a high counter separated a room filled with desks, currently unoccupied except for a couple officers. The nameplate on the counter read, "Sgt. Paul Nussbaum." I wondered, if these guys are usually called desk sergeants, does this make him a counter sergeant? I quickly decided that was a question best kept to myself.

"How can I help you?" Sergeant Nussbaum asked, unenthusiastically.

"We just saw the black Chevy pickup that was carjacked in Simmons Chapel," I told him.

"Ma'am," he said, smiling at us condescendingly, "Winston County is covered slap up with black Chevy pickups. What makes you so sure the one you saw was the stolen one?"

"This photo of the tag number, for one thing," Millie interjected, turning her phone screen toward the sergeant.

That got his attention. "Where'd you take this and when?" he demanded, suddenly interested in what we had to say.

"Less than ten minutes ago," Millie answered. "In back of Seafood King."

"Was anyone in the vehicle?" he asked.

"Apparently so," Millie said, "but I didn't realize it at first. The truck was kinda hidden behind the dumpster. When I walked to the back to take the photo, whoever was driving started the engine and took off."

"That wasn't a smart thing to do, ma'am," the sergeant scolded. "No telling what sort of character is driving that truck." Then, holding up his pointing finger to signal "hang on a sec," Sergeant Nussbaum pressed a button on the phone console and began speaking. "Ruby, get a BOLO out to all our patrols. The carjacked black Chevy pickup was spotted in the vicinity of Seafood King. And notify Fall Creek's people and the Troopers," he added, referring to the city police and the state's officers.

I'd read enough crime novels and watched enough police procedurals to know BOLO was an acronym for "be on the lookout." Surely, with every agency in the area looking for him, they'd be able to nab the truck thief in no time. I just prayed any chase wouldn't end up in the truck being wrecked. I really hoped it could be returned to Reverend Pratt in good condition.

Turning back to the two of us, Sergeant Nussbaum said, "We appreciate the information, ladies. Now let me get your names and contact information."

"And you'll let us know if you catch him?" I asked.

"I can't promise that, ma'am," he told me. "But if we have any other questions for either of you, we'll give you a call."

I knew a dismissal when I heard it, so Millie and I thanked the sergeant and headed back out to the sidewalk. "Nothing like a little consignment shopping to take our minds off all this criminal activity," I said as we crossed the side street en route to secondhand heaven.

6

Divine Consigns was my kind of shop. It, like its owners, twin sisters Iris and Irene Devine (with an E, but they used an "I" in the store name), had been around for ages. Iris and Irene were super selective about the merchandise they would accept, but, even so, they priced things reasonably.

The sales tags were imprinted with four prices and dates: the shop's original selling price and date the item was put into stock; 25 percent less and its 30th day's date; 50 percent less and it's 60th day's date; and then it got down to my spending level. After 90 days, the price was 75 percent less, with consignors having the option to pick up their unsold merchandise. Thirty days after that, anything not picked up went to a one-dollar rack for a short stint, and then, whatever didn't sell at that point was donated to a thrift store owned by a local charity.

The set of small brass bells on the entrance door jangled as we walked in. "Welcome," Iris or Irene called from behind the register.

I could never remember which one was who. Not surprising, since the ladies looked identical.

"Hi," I said. "You've remodeled since I was here last. I didn't see a sidewalk sale, so where can I find your best markdowns?" I'd learned years ago not to mind asking. After all, ask, and you just might receive a spectacular bargain. Don't ask, and you may miss out on the deal of a lifetime.

"Oh, it's you," Iris or Irene smiled. "I didn't recognize you at first, with the glare of the sun behind you. "The clearance section is loaded, and everything is buy two, get two free."

"Great," I said. "I'll see what I can find." I followed the ramp to a room about a fourth the size of the main showroom and started flipping through the racks of ladies' clothing. It didn't take me long to collect an armload to take to the dressing room. I'd hit the men's and children's sections after I'd narrowed down what I'd buy for myself.

"Here, hon," Iris or Irene said. "Let me take these and get a dressing room set up for you. Iris and I really do appreciate your mentioning our shop during your TV segment," she told me. "It's brought us quite a few new customers."

"I'm so glad to hear that," I responded. "If I find a place that offers really good deals, I'm certainly going to talk about it. I have a feeling I'll be showing off one of these bargains pretty soon," I said, nodding toward my stack of clothes Irene now had draped across her arm.

Now that I knew I was talking to Irene, I casually studied her features. I simply couldn't find one identifying mark that distinguished Irene from her sister. What I needed was a side-by-side comparison.

"Where is Iris?" I asked. "Are you working by yourself today?"

"No, she's here," Irene answered. "She's in the back tagging what's just come in. I'll let her know you're here. I know she'll want to speak to you too."

"Okay," I said as I closed the dressing room door.

Halfway through trying on all the tops I'd picked out, a tap sounded from the dressing room next to mine. "I may need your help with a zipper." Millie's voice sounded through the partition. "I may have caught it in the fabric."

"Hang on while I try this top on. I want to know what you think," I told her.

"Okay, I'm here," I called from Millie's doorway. The door swung inward and I eased through the opening.

Millie stood barefoot in a stunning purple and black color-blocked sheath dress. "Very pretty," I said. "Turn around and let me see if I can get the zipper loose."

Once I got the dress zipped, Millie did a slow twirl in front of the mirror. "Whatcha think?" she asked.

"It's you," I told her. "The colors, the style, the fit. Absolutely perfect."

"Flattery will get you a free Blizzard," Millie responded, smiling. "Now let me take a look at you."

The top I'd chosen was a long tunic in a mottled brown. I had several pairs of ankle-length and capri leggings that would coordinate well. Millie gave it a thumbs-up, so I went back to my cubicle, changed into my own clothes, and sauntered back to the clearance section to see what else I could find.

While Millie paid for her purchases, I chatted with a shopper who'd recognized me from my TV segments. I'd seen all kinds of reactions from people, from whispering behind my back, "Isn't that the lady on TV?" to more boisterous fans like Regina. This lady and I compared bargains and, as occasionally happens, she told me about another shop I'd never visited.

When I presented my stack of purchases, Iris greeted me warmly from her place behind the register, echoing her sister's thanks for my having mentioned their shop on TV. Irene stood at the other end of the counter, neatly folding each item to place them in one of their signature ribbon-decorated shopping bags.

"You found some of our best markdowns, as usual," Iris beamed.

"I sure did," I replied. "My husband is going to love the Carhartt jeans. I even found some sweet little outfits for my great niece Gracie. And I did buy three things for myself. But those two denim jackets and the long-sleeved tops are brand new. Still have the original tags on them. They're going to be Christmas presents."

It's always amazed me how often I've found brand new merchandise brought in by people who'd let clothes hang in their closet unworn instead of taking them back for a refund. The four new items I'd bought had already been noted beside names on my occasions list.

Even though it was summer, Christmas had a way of sneaking up on most folks. Then they ended up buying full price gifts on credit and still owing for them when the next Christmas came along. Not me. As my daddy often says, "A bargain's not a bargain unless you can afford it." And to me, that means never carry a credit balance. Sure, I keep a credit card for travel and I occasionally use it for online shopping, but the full balance is always paid every month.

Using cold, hard cash makes it much easier to limit your spending, so that's what I stick with most of the time. It's remarkable how much harder it is to turn loose of the green stuff than to simply pull out a piece of plastic.

I tried not to be conspicuous as I switched my view back and forth between the two sisters. Still, they were so much alike, I was at a loss to find a noticeable difference. Same face. Same build. Same eyes. Same hair color and style.

And then I spotted it. Irene, like me, was a lefty. She had handed me my bag of goodies using her left hand. And on said hand, there was a diamond solitaire the size of a hummingbird egg. Okay, maybe not quite that big, but a good three carats, I'd bet.

Iris, however, was probably a righty. She'd used her right hand to give me my receipt. Saying my goodbyes, I sneaked a peek at Iris's left hand. Its only adornment was a simple gold band. At last, I'd be able to call each lady by name.

"How are you going to remember who's who?" Millie asked when I told her about my discovery. "I mean, even if one's a lefty who wears a gold band ..."

"Egg-sized diamond," I corrected. "Lefty and diamond is Irene. Righty and gold band is Iris. And I may forget who's the lefty or righty, but I'll remember who's who because the longest name has the biggest ring. Ta-da! And Irene, diamond ring."

"Pretty good," Millie said. "And either or both of them could be ambidextrous, so stick with the Irene, diamond ring thing. Now what are we up to?"

"Let's cover a few blocks on foot and check out the shops. I especially want to find one that another shopper just told me about. She said it was only a couple blocks over. I Have Returned."

"Returned to what?" Millie asked.

"It's the store name," I explained, laughing. "They sell TV shopping channel items that were bought and returned, or were overstock. She said the discounts are really impressive."

"I'm about shopped out," Millie said. "And I can hear that Blizzard calling me."

"I don't plan to buy anything else," I said. "I just want to see what's here. Think of this as walking off those Blizzards before we eat them."

We must have wandered in and out of a half dozen small mom 'n' pop shops. I picked up business cards and hoped to come back and buy some things I could use for future TV segments. Even though viewers enjoyed seeing my bargains even when an item came from somewhere I traveled on vacation, it was especially nice when I could point them to a deal that was available within the viewing area. I'd recently mentioned a 10-dollar sidewalk sale at a new boutique in Bessemer and the sweet young lady who owned it sent me a Facebook message saying, the day of my segment, she'd sold every item in the sale before closing time.

Like Iris and Irene, small locally owned stores didn't have the budget to do much advertising, and some didn't even have websites, so getting a plug on TV could mean a real shot in the arm for business. I never played favorites, showing the best deals whether they were from big box stores, outlets, or places like these. But it always felt good when I could find a bargain that allowed me to mention one of the little guys.

Of course, shopping was not the only thing I talked about. And definitely not just clothes. I discovered a furniture outlet with exceptional prices and an unadvertised clearance room where pieces that'd worn out their welcome on the showroom floor were reduced to half-price, even if the item had already been drastically discounted. Case in point: out of that clearance room, I bought a $600 mirror marked down to $200. And at half the last markdown price, my final cost was $100.

I've passed along fabulous buys on vacation packages, appliances, school and office supplies, theme park and concert tickets, you-name-it. I've been asked how I find so many bargains, and I always reply that finding them is the easy part. Narrowing it down to the few I can cover in one segment is usually the problem.

When we reached I Have Returned, the Blizzards stopped calling so loudly as we admired row after row of neatly arranged merchandise. Jewelry, luggage, bedding, clothes, shoes. The place was loaded. Like moths to a flame, Millie and I wandered toward the back of the store, having learned long ago that if the fabulous deals weren't on the sidewalk or right in your face when you walked in, you could bet they were tucked away in the deepest, darkest corner.

Sure enough, the back left corner was stacked top to bottom with boxes of boots and the sign made me whip out my occasions list: "Your Choice: $20." Spring and summer were definitely the time to find boot bargains. And Dani, the granddaughter of Sammie, one of my besties, had a birthday coming up and I knew for a fact she'd been asking for boots. And not just any boots. The very boots in the box I was now holding.

I whipped out my phone and hit Sammie's number. "Have you already bought Dani any boots for her birthday?" I asked as soon as I heard her answer.

"I think her parents are going to have to buy them," Sammie said. "I've priced them, and they're somewhat out of my budget. Wish I could. Don't tell me you've found some at a bargain?"

"I have," I told her. "I'm standing here holding a box of black size six Beverly Heels right now. The style is called Townie. And—drum roll, please—they're twenty dollars."

"Twenty bucks!" Sammie exclaimed. "Those are the ones! Yes, yes, yes!" I got the impression she was excited.

"Hang on," I said. "I'm putting you on speaker and laying the phone down." Opening the box, I gave the boots a thorough exam, describing every detail.

"Thank you, thank you," Sammie said. "Dani's birthday is still three weeks away, so if I can owe you until we meet for lunch week after next, I can get the boots from you and pay you then."

"Deal," I said. I loved being the Bargainomics Lady. I'd made my dear friend very happy, and the boots were going to make her granddaughter ecstatic.

Our next stop was DQ, where we both slid into a booth and turned sideways to stretch our legs across our benches in most unladylike fashion. Thereafter, we proceeded to indulge in absolute ectasy. "Good thing we ordered small ones," I said, licking the last luscious drop from my spoon. "We'd need to cover a lot more blocks to walk off anything bigger."

"True," Millie agreed. "I say we go back to the house, take a swim, and then take the Sea-Doos out for a ride."

"It's Saturday," I reminded her. "Lots of boat traffic today and tomorrow. It might be better to put that off until Monday."

"Speaking of putting things off, we haven't even talked about our Norway trip, and we're leaving the week after Labor Day," Millie said.

Larry and I had been friends with the Nordstrands, a Norwegian family, for over twenty years. That many years ago, before I started doing TV, I was writing not only about Bargainomics, but also about any other topic that would put money in our bank account. Larry had taken photography lessons and had become a one-client photographer.

While covering the National Quartet Convention, I met and interviewed a trio, the Nordstrand Brothers, from Norway, who'd been invited to participate that year. The guys hadn't brought their wives, but Larry and I hit it off with the three brothers and stayed in touch. Three or four years later, I managed to get an assignment to cover the Gospel Music Convention in Peterhead, Scotland, where we met the wives, and all eight of us rented a van and spent a week wandering around Scotland after the Convention ended.

Our friendship had grown deeper through the years, and one particular couple, Per and Iren, the youngest brother and his wife, had become our regular traveling companions. We vacationed together every year, with me and Larry either going to Norway or meeting them somewhere in Europe, or them coming to the U.S. where we visited a different part of America together. The other two couples came over occasionally, and even some of the kids, who were now adults, came and visited.

Millie and Bill had met several of our Norwegian friends, but had never been to Norway. This was my and Larry's year to go there, and Millie, who needed no convincing, had finally talked Bill into making the trip.

"It's all under control," I said. "The tickets are ordered. Per and Iren are putting together some ideas for things to do, and you two are going to love it. That's all you need to know."

"But we leave really soon," Millie pointed out. "Less than two weeks," she said, holding up two fingers.

"And we'll set aside a full day to discuss all that as soon as we're back home. And we'll settle up on the cost of the tickets," I promised. "Right now we're lake people. Live in the moment," I said, crisscrossing my legs, holding my open palms up, and letting out a soft "om" sound.

"You don't do yoga," she said, laughing.

"No, but I look like I do yoga, don't I?" I said, closing my eyes and repeating my "om" sound.

"You look like a nut," she said. "And here comes some fans, O famous fruitcake."

I unfolded, greeting the couple who'd walked over to meet me. When they said their goodbyes, we went out the door behind them.

"When we said 'Let's make a day of it,' we succeeded," Millie said. "It's nearly five o'clock. Should we swing by the sheriff's station and see if anyone's located that pickup?"

"Nah," I said. "They probably wouldn't tell us if they had."

"Oh, just pull up out front and I'll run in and ask our good buddy Sergeant Nussbaum," Millie said.

"Well, that was unenlightening," Millie declared as she climbed back into the Hyundai. "I'm beginning to suspect Sergeant Nussbaum wouldn't have told me if he'd had the truck thieves trussed up on the floor behind the counter."

"You're probably right," I agreed. "Let's get back to Jane's and indulge in some reading and porch time. Then we can stay up late and watch a movie or read some more. Or go fishing."

"No fishing for me," Millie said. "We are planning to go to church tomorrow morning, aren't we?"

"Of course," I said. "Did you have somewhere in particular in mind?"

"Why don't we visit Simmons Chapel?" she suggested. "It's close by, and we might get to ask Reverend Pratt a few questions."

"Why, you sneaky dickens," I exclaimed. "Am I rubbing off on you, or is it vice versa?"

We both cracked up laughing. Our family was filled with crime readers, crime solvers, and even a few crime committers. Millie's mom and mine had exchanged *True Detective* and *True Crime* magazines, which they'd kept hidden from children's eyes underneath their mattresses. Whenever Millie was at my family's house, we'd sneak Mother's out and read ourselves terrified. Ditto for when I went to Millie's.

Now, as adults, we had a morbid curiosity about homicides and crime in general. Our cousin Jim had retired after a lifetime of service on the police force, from motorcycle cop to sheriff of the county. Two more cousins, Eric and Matt, were cops in Birmingham and Shelby County, respectively.

We couldn't help ourselves. Crime was in our bloodline. Doubly so in mine. Which also explained Cousin Valerie, who was currently doing a nickel, as they say in the big house, for embezzling enough money for an in-ground pool, a vacation to Bali for her entire family of six, and a donation to her eldest daughter Shannon's private school that secured the graceless girl a starring role in the school's performance of "Grease."

It was impossible to wrap my head around the idea of the chubby, acned Shannon as Sandy, the part that'd been played by Olivia Newton-John in the movie. Fortunately, fate intervened. Valerie was arrested and Shannon's headlining part was quickly handed off to her understudy, Alyssa Buckner, a petite blonde and the girlfriend of Nathan Slovensky, who was playing Danny, John Travolta's character. Nathan was undoubtedly euphoric over the role reassignment.

Truthfully, I don't believe Shannon ever wanted the part in the first place. Shannon, like Millie and so many other family members who had selfishly absorbed all the artistic genes, happily jumped into the role of set director and did a job worthy of the rave review *The Birmingham News* saw fit to give the school's production. Consequently, Shannon caught the eyes of the powers-that-be at the Alabama Shakespeare Festival and she is now one of their top set designers. Plus, she's lost her baby fat, cleared up her skin, and found a career that she says she was made for.

7

Rounding a tight curve, a rundown roadside flea market appeared almost directly in front of me. I made a slight swerve and whipped into the rutted dirt turn-in.

"You could've given me a little warning there, cuz," Millie said, grabbing hold of the safety handle above her window.

"Sorry," I said. "I'd forgotten this was here. I promise this'll be our last stop. Except for the Super Center."

"Looks pretty seedy," Millie said. The building was an ancient converted chicken house.

"One man's trash …" I said. "Remember that lady who bought the Jackson Pollock for almost nothing at a flea market? Turned out worth millions. I'm still looking for mine."

"I've never been a Pollock fan," Millie said. "Abstract impressionism I can deal with, to a point, but 'drip painting'? No, if I want paint dripped, I'll go get my grandkids."

"If I'd found that painting," I said, "I'd have adored it all the way to Sotheby's. And I'd continue to think fondly of Mr. Pollock as I spent my cool millions."

The building was about 100 feet long and divided into numbered 10-foot sections manned by different sellers, except for a spot where one seller had taken a double space. This late in the afternoon, though, most of the booths were already covered with sheets or tarps and the sellers long gone. The few remaining shoppers were either headed out the door or finishing up their purchases.

"Looks like we missed most of it," I said. "Since we're here, let's walk on through."

"In case there's an Andy Warhol hiding back there somewhere?" Millie teased.

"Norman Rockwell, maybe," I said. "I don't think these are Warhol kind of people."

As we reached the farthest end of the building, a heavyset, overall-clad man of indeterminate years was leaning forward on his table and calling to us. "Ladies," he said, his speech hesitant and nasal, "c'mere. I got some nice things and good prices." He waved a hand to show off his display.

Millie and I gave each other a look, immediately perceiving that the man, most likely, had a learning disability. A hand-printed cardboard sign thumbtacked to the wall behind him read, "Cooter's Colectables."

This is where I have to make a confession. I'm one of the grammar police. I try to restrain myself, but sometimes it's irresistible. I'd already struggled no end with c-o-l-l-e-c-t-a-b-l-e-s having become an acceptable spelling for *collectibles*. But this? I longed for a permanent marker. Millie, knowing what I was thinking, nudged my foot with hers and shot me a warning glance.

Cooter neither smelled nor looked particularly clean. A brown liquid had made a permanent stain in the crease running from the corner of his mouth to his chin. A matching stain was on the bib of his overalls, and as he smiled, his toothless mouth gave us a clear view of the massive wad of tobacco packed into his cheek.

"Looka here," he said, picking up a rusted knife with a broken blade. "I fount this out in the woods. 'At's where I find mosta my stuff," he said, warming to his subject. "I got arrowheads, purty rocks, squirrel tails, driftwood, pine cones—you can make a lot of purty things with driftwood and pine cones—and I've even got some fossils." He lifted a piece of gray slate bearing the black imprint of an eons-old fern.

"That's really special," Millie told him. "You do have some nice things."

"Name's Cooter," he said, extending a grimy hand with Lord-knows-what encrusted beneath his fingernails. "What's y'all's names?"

Ignoring the hand, Millie said, "I'm Millie, and this," she nodded toward me, "is my cousin Judy."

"Cousins," he said. "I thought y'all was sisters." He reached under his table and pulled out his spittoon, a blue plastic Maxwell House coffee container, which he then used. And had obviously been using for a month or two without emptying. He used the back of his hand to wipe the excess dribble from his face before tucking a fresh glob of tobacco into his cheek.

"We get that a lot," I said, although it baffled both of us, since we saw no resemblance whatsoever.

"I ain't never seen y'all here," Cooter said. "Y'all not from around here?"

"No, we're not," I said, "but we're staying at a friend's house on Smith Lake."

"Smith Lake!" Cooter said. "I go to the lake a lot. Don't live far from it. Where 'bouts y'all stayin'?"

I wasn't comfortable with giving Cooter our exact location, so I simply responded, "About an hour from here." That seemed to satisfy him.

"What y'all lookin' for?" Cooter asked.

Millie winked at me, then leaned in conspiratorially toward Cooter. "If you can keep a secret, I'll tell you," she said.

Just as Millie had figured, the idea of sharing a secret delighted Cooter. "I can keep a secret with the best of 'em," he said. "Cross my heart and hope to die," he added, making the sign across the bib of his overalls as he spoke.

"We're treasure hunters," Millie said. "And we're hoping to find a treasure right here in this flea market."

Cooter was momentarily stunned into silence. "What kinda treasure are y'all lookin' for?" he asked, his voice lowered in awe.

"We look for all different kinds of treasure," I told him.

"Paintings. Books. I might even buy one of these rocks you have here. I think there are all kinds of treasure, don't you?"

"I sure do," he said, getting more excited.

"How much do you want for this piece of gold?" I asked, pointing to a fist-sized chunk of pyrite.

"I'll take five dollars for it," Cooter said. "But I gotta be honest wif you. That ain't real gold." He watched my face to see if I looked disappointed.

"That's all right," I said. "It's very pretty and I like it." I pulled out a 10-dollar bill and handed it to him. "Matter of fact, I like it 10 dollars' worth."

Cooter's jaw dropped, but before he could recover his powers of speech, Millie pointed to another piece of pyrite. "I need my own pyrite treasure," she said. Elbowing me and grinning at her own pun, she said, "Pyrite. Pirate. Treasure. Get it?"

"Yes, I get it," I said. "Very funny."

Cooter found his voice. "I've had a lot of people talk me down on my prices, but I ain't never had nobody pay me more than I was askin'," he said. "Y'all sure are nice."

"Well, we think you're nice too, Cooter," I told him. And we did. Dirt, tobacco, and all. Cooter had already grown on us, and it felt good to be able to help him put some extra cash in his pocket.

Unzipping the pouch of his overalls' bib, he tucked away the twenty dollars and pulled a paper bag from a five-gallon plastic bucket on the floor beside him. "If it's all right, I'm gonna put both y'all's treasures into one sack. That'll save me havin' to use an extry one," Cooter explained, opening the sack and gently placing the first rock inside it.

"Sure," Millie said.

"They call this pyrite *fool's gold*," Cooter said. "But I know about real gold too." He lowered his voice almost to a whisper. "Y'all told me your secret. Now I'm gonna tell you mine," he said. "But first, y'all got to do the promise."

We glanced around, trying not to smile since this was, for Cooter, a very serious moment. "Cross our hearts and hope to die," Millie and I said, simultaneously signing crosses on our chests.

Cooter motioned for us to come behind his table. He pulled his bucket of paper bags from the stack of buckets beneath it, flipped three buckets upside down, and offered seats to me and Millie. Crust of filth aside, Cooter was a gentleman. He waited until Millie and I were both seated before taking his own seat.

As quickly as he sat, he stood again, doing a final sweep for eavesdroppers. Seeing no one, Cooter returned to his bucket. "They's treasure in Smith Lake," he solemnly told us. "And I figger, y'all being treasure hunters and all, you might want to know about it."

"Oh, we do," Millie assured him.

"The story goes back a long, long time. Back to the Korean War. Back before there even was a Smith Lake," Cooter began.

"There was a man named Henry Dixon what lived up thisaway. Whilst he was still in Korea, he took to sending all these dolls and statues home. His wife would get packages all the time, and ever' time she opened one, it'd be another of them dolls. Not the kind kids play with, mind you. China, I guess you'd call 'em.

"Strange to keep sendin' dolls when him and his wife didn't have no girl. They had a boy. And boys don't tend to care much for dolls and such. Anyhow, when he come home, he seen his wife had strung those dolls and such across their mantelpiece and, for whatever reason, he didn't like that one bit. He brung his duffel bag into the living room and starting rakin' them dolls off into the bag. When he had ever' one of 'em throwed in the bag, he slammed out the door and was gone all night. When he come back the next mornin', he didn't have them dolls and nobody ever' seen 'em again."

"Didn't his wife ask him about them?" I interjected.

"She was prob'ly afraid to. Henry mighta had a touch o' that STP or whatever they call it these days. You know, when your mind's got messed up by all the stuff you seen while you was fightin'."

We nodded, but didn't correct or interrupt.

"Whatever was the matter with him, he took to hangin' out at a juke joint not far from his house. They sold moonshine and I hear tell there was a lot of other stuff what went on there, but I won't tell none of that in the comp'ny of ladies.

"Well, one night, he was more'n three sheets in the wind and was walkin' home from the joint. Just as a car come by, he stumbled and fell right out in front of it. There he lay, barely alive. A ambulance come, and as they was loadin' him in, his wife showed up and run over to him.

'I'm a goner,' he told her. "But you and the boy is took care of. Everything you need is in Swaller Canyon'."

"So what was he talking about?" I asked him.

"That's just it. Don't nobody know. Or least, nobody used to. His wife tried and tried to figger out what he was talkin' about. All they knowed was it was something to do with them dolls. She and the boy searched all over Swaller Canyon until they couldn't get in there no more."

"Why couldn't they get in there?" I asked.

"'Cause it got flooded. Swaller Canyon's part of Smith Lake now," Cooter told us. "All that land is under the water. And that boy, James, even joined the Navy and got trained to be a frogman just so's he could keep on lookin'. Then James' own boy got old enough to start lookin', but he didn't have no luck either. But he had a son too, and he's the fourth generation tryin' to find the treasure." Cooter paused to spit a brown stream into his Maxwell House spittoon.

"So Henry's great-grandson is the one looking now?" Millie asked.

"That he is," said Cooter. "And a whole lotta other folks too. They's always been people lookin' for that treasure and they might always will be."

"It would certainly help if someone had an idea of what the treasure really is," I said.

"I know what it is," Cooter said, matter-of-factly.

"You do?" Millie asked. "Is that your secret? You found the treasure?"

"Not 'zactly," he said. "But I know what it is now."

"You do?" I said. "How do you know?"

"It's gold," he said, his voice at a whisper.

"Gold?" Millie said. "How did you find out what it is?" She and I exchanged glances, confirming we were both highly skeptical.

"It were a miracle," he said. "You ever read where Jesus sent Peter fishin' to come up with the money to pay His and Peter's taxes?" Cooter asked.

"Matthew 17," I said.

"Then you know what happened," Cooter said. "Peter caught a fish and opened up its mouth, and there was the money to pay their taxes!"

"That was definitely a miracle," I said, encouraging him to continue.

"Well, pert near the same thing happened to me. I was fishin' over by Swaller Point …"

I butted in. "Swallow Point?" I asked. "Would this be the same area as Swallow Canyon?"

"Sure 'nuf," he said. "Swaller Point is a tad west of what was the mainest part of Swaller Canyon, but it ain't far away a'tall."

"As I was sayin'," Cooter said, taking a moment to spit toward, but not exactly in, his coffee container, "it was just gettin' dusky dark. If you don't night fish, evenin' is a pretty good time too. It ain't so hot, and the fish usually bite pretty good.

"I'd been fishin' for prob'bly an hour when this big ol' catfish hit my line. I knowed it was a catfish because it toyed with my line s'long before it finally took it under. You can always tell a catfish that way," he nodded, sagely. "Less'n you're fishin' around a mess of little bream," he added. "Now them things will knock the fire out of your bait. Play with it 'til they clean the last dab off your hook. But they never pull your cork under. They can't, see. Too dang little."

Millie and I didn't want to be rude to poor Cooter, but this story was turning into a saga, and we had to pick up a few groceries and we wanted to be back at the lake house well before dark.

"But you knew what it was when that big catfish took your cork under," Millie said, hoping to move the story along.

"I shore did," Cooter said. "I'd figgered on catchin' me enough to eat on for a day or two. Maybe five or six channel cats. But when I commenced to pullin' this 'un up, a head the size of a cantaloupe come up out of that water. It was a big ol' blue cat, and I'm bettin' it'd go 30 pounds or better."

"Wow!" we both said, truly impressed.

"But, shoot, that ain't nothin'," Cooter continued. "They's a blue cat caught outa Holt Reservoir over toward Tuscaloosa that weighed more'n 120 pounds," Cooter informed us.

"My goodness!" I said, as Millie let out another "Wow!"

"Yep," Cooter nodded. "But my catfish had something none of these other 'uns had."

"What's that?" Millie asked.

"Gold," Cooter whispered in a voice tinged with amazement. "I started cleanin' him and I always like to see what a fish has been eatin'," he said. "A lot of people call me 'Crazy Cooter,' but I ain't crazy and I ain't nearly as dumb as some folks think I am."

"You aren't crazy or dumb, Cooter," I assured him, tempted, but restraining myself, from patting the knee of his nasty britches.

"Thank you," he said, shyly.

"Anyhow, like I said," Cooter went on, "I like to see what a fish has been eatin', 'cause if you know what they's been eatin', you know what kind of bait can catch 'em." He grinned with pride at his logic.

"That's really smart," I said, truthfully. I think Cooter blushed at that, but it was hard to tell through the dirt layer.

"So I'm sortin' through what I find: some bass, bream, what looked like a piece of a beaver tail, a silver pop top—they like shiny things—and then I seen it." He looked at us both, obviously enjoying his moment and the building suspense.

"What was it?" I asked. I was no longer faking interest. Cooter had reeled me into his story and hooked me.

"A piece of gold," Cooter said, triumphantly.

"Really!" Millie said. "That's amazing! What did you do with it?"

He scanned the building while surreptitiously unzipping the pocket of his overalls' bib. "I got it right here," he said, and extracted a shiny lump of what appeared to be honest-to-goodness gold. "Wanna hold it?" he asked.

"I do," I said, forgetting all about Cooter's cooties and nastiness.

The thin piece of metal was perhaps a quarter-inch thick and a misshapen circle of maybe two inches diameter. I squeezed as hard as I could and felt the metal give beneath my fingers. I was no assayer, but I'd bet my next Blizzard I was holding a piece of genuine pure gold. I passed it to Millie for her to examine.

"So you think this catfish swallowed Dixon's treasure?" Millie asked as she studied Cooter's prized possession before handing it back to him.

"Naw," Cooter snorted. "That's just a teeny little ol' piece of it," he said, returning the gold to his bib pouch. "They's bunches more where that come from."

"How do you know that?" I asked.

"I just know," Cooter said, growing uncomfortable. "I done said too much."

"Well, your secret is safe with us, Cooter. We won't tell anyone else," I promised. "But we might try our luck at catfishing," I joked.

"Fish all you want," Cooter said, "but they ain't but one place where you're likely to catch one swimmin' around with another piece o' gold inside."

"Swallow Point?" Millie asked.

"Aw, dang it," Cooter said, yanking off his cap and slapping his knee with it. "I done said way too much."

I started to touch his shoulder, but thought better of it. "Cooter," I said, meeting his gaze as seriously as I could, "we won't try to catch any catfish and we won't tell anybody about your gold. But we want you to make us another promise too."

"What's that?" Cooter asked, replacing his cap over a head of greasy brown hair and propping his hands on his knees.

"We don't want you to show anyone else your gold," I told him. "There are some bad people in this world, and gold is very valuable. If one of those people knew you had it, they might try to take it away from you."

"And they might even hurt you to get it," Millie said. "We like you, Cooter, and we wouldn't want anything bad to happen to you."

"I ain't told nary a soul," Cooter vowed, "'cept'n for y'all and my friend Antoine. And Antoine told me the same thing. He said not to tell nobody."

"That was very wise of him," I said, not bothering to point out that he'd ignored Antoine's advice when he'd told us about the gold piece.

The lights in the other end of the building went off and we all three stood to our feet. "Looks like it's closing time," I said.

"Yep," said Cooter. "I shore did enjoy talkin' to y'all. Most folks don't have time for ol' Cooter. Y'all are really nice ladies."

"We think you're nice too," Millie told him. Then, throwing caution to the wind, Millie gave Cooter the lightest and fastest hug on record. Or at least, if the Guinness people had seen it, I've no doubt it'd been a winner.

Cooter walked us to the door and watched us climb into the car. There was a momentary pause while we shared a bottle of hand sanitizer, and then we were off. Cooter waved and smiled his toothless smile and we returned the wave and the smile, teeth added.

"What an unexpected friendship," Millie said. "With a bar of soap and some breath mints, Cooter could be downright endearing. And he was pretty sweet, dirt and all."

"He really was," I agreed. "I so hope he realizes how important it is not to talk about that gold. If it's real—and I think we both are pretty certain it is—he's got several thousand dollars hidden away in those overalls."

"Do you really believe he got that gold out of a catfish?" Millie asked.

"I do," I said. "Catfish are bottom feeders, and not too particular about what they eat. A shiny piece of gold lying on the bottom of the lake probably looked quite tasty to Mr. Catfish."

"But how do you suppose it got there?" Millie persisted. "And do you think it's really part of the treasure Henry Dixon stashed in Swallow Canyon?"

"I think we're going to have to do some research," I said.

"Let's get our Blizzards to go and enjoy the porch until dark," Millie said. "Then we can go in and get on the internet."

"An excellent plan there, cuz," I said.

8

I had picked up a bag of lemons at the Super Center, so our first task upon returning to the lake house was to find the juicer I was confident Jane had. Top shelf, pantry. Jane was so well organized.

I pulled out two tall slender acrylic glasses and decorated the lip of each one with a generous slice of lemon. I placed them on the tray with an ice-filled pitcher of my freshly squeezed lemonade, carried the tray to the porch, and set it on a low table between the two chaise lounges.

"And," said Millie, plopping into each glass a wooden skewer of pineapple and mango chunks interspersed with bright red stemless cherries, "a little more garnish for our lemonade."

"A work of art," I declared.

After an hour or two buried in our books, we both decided our Blizzards were not holding up as expected. "Keep reading," Millie said. "I'll whip up a little something to sustain us."

Two chapters later, Millie appeared with a tray of finger sandwiches encircling a brimming bowl of strawberries and cheese cubes on toothpicks. I plucked my bookmark off the table and stuck it into *Murder in July.* "You've outdone yourself!" I exclaimed. The crusts had been neatly trimmed away—something Larry would have considered a crime since he was the ultimate crust lover—and each small triangle was perfectly angled to form a lovely and tasty display.

"Cucumber, pimento cheese, seafood salad," Millie said, pointing to one of each selection. "Bon appétit. "

For booklovers, few things can compete with finger food you can eat while continuing to read. The ceiling fans overhead kept a perfect breeze wafting over us, and only the distant sound of boats and other watercraft broke the silence.

"Hard to believe this is the same place where we ran inside and all but barricaded ourselves in last night," Millie said.

"I know," I agreed. "It seems downright ridiculous in the light of day."

"We really do have overactive imaginations," Millie said.

"And here's part of the reason," I said, holding up my book and giving a nod toward Millie's.

"But it sure is fun, isn't it?" Millie said.

"Yeah, it is," I agreed. "I can't imagine not being a reader."

We read until the natural light made it impossible. By then, the crickets, frogs, and whippoorwills had assembled quite an orchestra, with the occasional owl adding a hoot or two.

"I guess that's the biggest advantage to electronic books," Millie said, noisily slapping her book shut. "If we were using our tablets, we could stay right here and keep reading."

"That, and being able to take dozens of books on a trip in a space no bigger than one book," I said. "Even so, I'm old school. There's something wonderful about turning an actual page to see what happens next."

By the time Millie opened the bathroom door, I was already ensconced on my side of the bed, pillows piled high behind me and my laptop fired up and ready. "I know you're never without a pad and pencil, so round them up and prepare to take notes," I instructed.

My first search was for the name Henry Dixon. Google only offered 42,400,000 results for that. I tried again, this time adding Fall Creek and Alabama to the search criteria.

Bingo. *"The search for Dixon's Treasure,"* I read. "Here's an old newspaper article from the *Fall Creek Chronicle.*" Millie scooted closer and began to read along with me.

June 3, 1971. In 1953, Henry Dixon's dying words to his wife hinted of valuables concealed somewhere in Swallow Canyon. Eight years later, the chances of finding Dixon's mysterious treasure were literally drowned when Swallow Canyon became part of the gigantic Alabama Power reservoir, Lewis Smith Lake.

More than one treasure-seeking diver has lost his life searching for this supposed fortune. This week, three young boys, ages 13, 14, and 16 were rescued by a passing boater after the teens' inflatable raft sank, leaving the three struggling to reach the distant shoreline.

When questioned by the Alabama Marine Patrol, the boys, who were all wearing swim googles, said they had been trying to swim to the bottom and search for Dixon's Treasure. None of the boys had brought along a life jacket, and their parents had no idea the boys were even in the water.

'It's insane,' said one boy's father, who asked not to be identified. 'These rumors about the Dixon Treasure were going around when I was their age. It's a fable, nothing more. As long as people keep telling it, kids like these, and adults too, are going to put their lives at risk chasing something that doesn't exist.'

"You can't blame that dad for being upset or saying it was a hoax," Millie said. "He almost lost his child, and he'd heard the same story when he was a kid, and nothing had ever come of it."

I went back to the search results and clicked another selection. This article was more recent—2014. It covered more of the information Cooter had given us, although not nearly as colorfully or grammatically incorrect. As I scanned through the paragraphs, the name Harriet Dixon caught my attention.

"Look here," I said to Millie, indicating the paragraph I'd moved to the top of the screen.

Asked whether or not she believed the treasure to be legitimate, Harriet Dixon Maske responded, 'My first husband, James, was fixated on finding that treasure. And when he couldn't, he started looking for other ones he'd heard about. If it wasn't for that one word, I wouldn't have become a widow before I was 40,' said Mrs. Maske.

'I didn't want to lose my son like I did my husband. I never talked about the treasure to him. Of course, he's a grown man now, and a lot of people have asked him about it. But he's the third generation since that whole tale got started. If there really was one, someone would have found it by now.'

"Those weren't very helpful," I said. "Let's see if we can find any military records about Henry Dixon. If we start at the beginning, we might find a clue as to what, if anything, Dixon actually shipped home besides dolls."

This time, I searched Henry Dixon and Alabama and South Korea. A minute or so later, we were reading through a journal uploaded by the son of Army Lieutenant Mack Falco. Since letters to home and any other forms of written communication generally ended up heavily redacted, Falco had secretly maintained the journal and managed to safely bring it and himself back to the States.

Throughout his stint in South Korea, and at the point where I spotted Henry Dixon's name, Falco was serving as platoon leader in the Boseong region of South Jeolla Province. He mentioned fields of green tea leaves and some issues with local villagers, and then a single sentence, a sort of sidebar: *Sarge thinks this new corporal, Henry Dixon, is a bad influence on the men.*

"What's that supposed to mean?" Millie asked.

"Got me," I said.

My next search was for South Korea and Boseong and South Jeolla and stolen. "Jackpot!" I yelled. "Listen to this."

It seems unlikely that even a North Korean would desecrate a Buddhist temple. Therefore, American soldiers have remained at the top of the suspect list. It has been confirmed that U.S. troops were active in the area when a statue of the mountain god Sanshin, made up of approximately 60 pounds of pure gold, disappeared from a Buddhist temple in Boseong.

It was Millie's time to yell. "That's it! Henry Dixon stole that gold statue."

"And somehow broke it down into small enough pieces to ship home bit by bit inside all those dolls and figurines," I said. "Cooter's story is beginning to make a whole lot of sense."

"I wish we knew how to scuba dive," Millie said. "Maybe we could find Dixon's gold. And if we did, we'd share it with Cooter."

"Divers!" I exclaimed. "I bet that's what those two we saw Friday were doing."

"Possibly," Millie said, "but as you pointed out yourself, a lot of people dive Smith Lake. I doubt they're all looking for Dixon's Treasure."

"But not all of them are diving in Swallow Canyon, either," I countered. "And Cooter's fish had to have come from somewhere near here, which means there's gold in that thar canyon!"

"So what are we gonna do about it?" Millie asked excitedly.

"I don't know," I said. "But even if we found it, it'd only be right to give it back to South Korea."

"They want a statue back, not a pile of gold pieces," Millie argued.

"Think about what you're saying," I said. "Can you imagine how much money 60 pounds of gold would be worth? Even if we couldn't return the actual statue, the gold that used to be the statue still belongs to South Korea."

"Oh, fine," Millie grumbled, "have a conscience. I'd rather have the gold."

"No, you hadn't," I chided, "and you know it. You wouldn't enjoy that ill-gotten gain, knowing you should have returned it to its rightful owner."

"Couldn't I at least enjoy a world cruise before I started to feel guilty?" Millie asked.

"Gee, I don't know. Maybe you should check with Cousin Valerie. I'm sure she could answer that question."

"I repent," Millie said, hanging her head. "I had a momentary lapse, thinking of all that money."

"We really do need to go to church in the morning," I laughed.

"And we really need to get some sleep if we plan to get there," Millie said.

I turned back to my laptop, preparing to shut it down. "Listen to this," I said. "It's the final paragraph in the article: *One wealthy South Korean businessman, Jae-geun Yi, has maintained an offer currently equivalent to 50,000 U.S. dollars for the return of the statue.*"

"So you think Mr. Yi will give us 50,000 bucks for the bits and pieces of that statue?" Millie asked.

"You know what I always say," I reminded her. "Don't be afraid to ask. The worst thing they can tell you is 'No'."

"Well, as soon as we find it, I'm calling Mr. Yi," Millie said. "Fifty thousand is better than nothing."

"That's the spirit," I said, placing my laptop on the nightstand. "After church, we'll start working on a way to train a giant catfish to lead us to the treasure."

"Like a bloodhound," Millie said. "Only following the scent of gold."

Neither of us received any nighttime revelations about finding the gold, but we did get our best night of uninterrupted sleep. We were up early enough to enjoy some quality time on the porch before heading off to Simmons Chapel.

When we arrived at the church, the parking lot was almost full. "Either Reverend Pratt has an extraordinarily faithful following," Millie commented, "or they're outgrowing their facilities."

"Or a lot of extra people are coming to show their support and encouragement," I suggested.

"Or like us, they want to be supportive and nosy," Millie said.

"I'm sure that's true," I responded.

At the bottom of the steps leading into the sanctuary, a pretty brunette in a super cute three-quarter sleeve blue floral top and royal blue midi skirt greeted us. Millie and I looked at each other's ankle pants and prayed we weren't walking into a place that frowned on women wearing pants. She and I had had that displeasure before.

A year or so back, a church in Florida had invited me to speak about Biblical money management, the very heart of Bargainomics, and I'd worked it out so, instead of paying my plane fare, they paid for a rental car and fuel so that Millie would be able to come with me. I'd spoken on Saturday evening and had another speaking engagement near home on the following Monday, so it was imperative that we start toward home first thing Sunday morning.

We'd been doing this for years, so we'd developed a routine for when we were on the road on Sundays. Occasionally, we did an internet search and knew ahead of time where we'd be stopping for church, but typically, around 10:00 a.m., we began watching along our route for a church we could visit.

On this particular Sunday, we spotted a cheery-looking small brick church set upon a small rise—a mountain by Florida standards—and bearing the name of Friendship. "This is it," we both agreed, and I turned into the drive, parked, and we joined the rest of the people entering the building.

Inside, an usher welcomed us, handing each of us an order of service. His smile faded as quickly as it had appeared as he stared down at our pants-covered legs. Immediately, our eyes swept over the congregation and, to our chagrin, we realized every woman in the building was either wearing a dress or a skirt. Not only that, but every eye that wasn't staring straight at us was cast down as if to keep the horrifying image of our pants legs blocked from their memory.

Not another soul spoke to us, save for that solitary usher. After the service, we left as quickly as we could. At the door, one lady put out a hand and caught my elbow. "I'm glad you were here," she said sincerely. Millie and I were both quite sure she was the only one.

And then there was that occasion when a coworker of Larry's invited us to a special Tuesday evening service at his church—I should have learned from that one. Larry and I walked into the church, Bibles in hand, spotted Larry's friend and his wife already seated in one of the pews, and made our way over to them. The man's wife looked up and, seeing my pants legs, began frantically whispering to her husband on her left and the person on her right.

Before Larry and I reached their pew, the people had spaced themselves out to guarantee two more folks couldn't squeeze in. Larry and I took a seat on another pew where we sat completely ignored throughout the service and afterward. Larry's coworker hightailed it out the back door while we made a hasty and humiliated retreat to our car.

Which is why, sometime after that, when a woman from a church I wasn't familiar with phoned and asked me to speak, I went through the series of questions I'd developed to help avoid unpleasant situations. More importantly, it had never been my intention to ignore or insult any church's customs and I hoped to avoid even inadvertently being offensive.

"Have you been on my website?" I asked.

"Oh, yes," she said. "That's one of the reasons we wanted to have you here."

"And you've seen my photo?" I asked. "You know I have short hair and wear jewelry, makeup, and pants."

"I watch your WEEE segments every time you're on," she vowed.

And so the date was set. Sidekick Millie went with me as my Vanna White. I usually brought along a number of show 'n' tell items and Millie would model some of the clothes and walk around the audience showing the price tags of other bargains from men's and kids' clothes to tools, jewelry, and home goods.

Waiting to be introduced, Millie and I were seated at a table with the pastor's wife and the women's ministry leader, the lady who had invited me. "You go ahead and do the introduction," the pastor's wife said to the other lady.

Other lady replied to the pastor's wife, "I'd rather you did it."

And then the bomb dropped. "I'm not going to introduce her," the pastor's wife said, with enough sourness in her voice to have been sucking on lemons. "You're the one who invited her." Apparently the two had forgotten we were sitting right there during this entire exchange.

My inviter reluctantly and half-heartedly introduced me, and her enthusiasm carried to the rest of those present. Throughout what became one of the shortest presentations of my career, I could visualize the entire audience, eyes closed, fingers in their ears, chanting, "La, la, la, la, la" to keep from hearing me.

To this day, I have no explanation for their attitude that night, but—not that I'm saying one is connected with the other—the honest-to-goodness truth is that church was struck by lightning a few weeks later and burned completely to the ground. Just saying.

But for those few bad experiences, I've had countless wonderful ones. I've made forever friends and met some of the sweetest people on this planet.

Guess that's why I've never understood why a person will allow one bad experience to sour them on church. I mean, if one church isn't the one for you, go next door. At least, here in the South, there's a church on every corner.

Speaking of sweet people, at a church in California, I was on my own since driving hadn't been an option and buying Millie a ticket simply wasn't in the budget. At the church, there were several hundred ladies present and I was delighted to see a full range of ages from teens to super seniors.

"Bargains are everywhere," I'd said as part of my wrap-up. "It's simply a matter of knowing how to find them." I began showing some of the items I'd managed to cram into my luggage. My books and other materials had been shipped ahead of me.

My initial reception had been wonderfully warm and, after my presentation, these charming ladies had come up to me in droves, thanking me, telling me their own bargain-shopping adventures, and examining my show 'n' tells. Carol, the church's women's ministry leader, and I have stayed in touch ever since. Larry and I have traveled back to California to visit with them, and she and her husband Rocky, have come to Alabama to visit us. The friendships I've made in so many different places are the best part of sharing Bargainomics.

At a church in rural Georgia, a silver-haired super senior with a sturdy bun knotted at the back of her head had picked up a pair of burgundy patent wedge sandals I'd used as part of my show 'n' tell and was giving them the once-over.

"Where did you say you found these?" she asked. Her big blue eyes sparkled through thick wire-rimmed lenses and her print dress, cotton sweater, support hose, and orthopedic shoes reminded me so much of Larry's maternal grandmother.

"In Scotland," I said, admittedly rather condescendingly. This dear lady had, most likely, never been out of Georgia.

"In what city?" she persisted.

"Dundee," I said, a patient smile plastered on my face.

"Oh, such a beautiful place, Dundee," she said. "And of course, Saint Andrews. And Edinburgh," she added.

I failed to hide the surprise on my face. "You've been there?" I asked.

"Oh, my, yes. Many times," she responded. "During my career, I traveled extensively all over the world."

"You did?" I said, and quickly added, "You must have had a

wonderful job. What did you do?" I certainly didn't want this kindly lady to realize I doubted her truthfulness.

"I was in the Secret Service," she said, no hint of humor in her voice.

If I'd just taken a drink from my water bottle, I'd have given said lady a shower. "Really!" I responded, wanting to kick myself. Every word that came out of my mouth let her know I was having trouble buying her story. "What did you do?" I fully expected her to say, "If I told you that, I'd have to kill you."

"Not in the kind of position most people think of," she said, matter-of-factly. "I was the massage therapist for the Kennedy family."

"The Kennedy family?" I asked. "*The* Kennedy family, as in JFK and Jackie?"

"The very ones," she smiled. "Such precious people. But President Kennedy could tie his back into knots whenever he was golfing. When we were at Saint Andrews, I had my work cut out for me. Of course, he always had a terrible time with his back, poor man." Saint Andrews, I knew, was considered the oldest golf course in the world and one that every golf enthusiast had on his bucket list.

"What were they like?" I asked, my mind already thinking what a great article I could get from this delightfully unexpected encounter.

"Oh, I couldn't tell you that," she smiled, a faraway look hinting of her treasure trove of memories. "If I did …"

This time I was sure I was about to hear, "I'd have to kill you," as I pictured Larry's grandma's lookalike aiming a SIG-Sauer at my head. But that wasn't where she was headed.

"... I'd break a sacred oath," she said. "I swore to never discuss the Kennedy family, and I never will. I enjoyed every minute I had with them, and my memories will go with me when I leave this old world," she finished.

Yeah, I've come across a few bad apples, but those experiences are far outweighed by the kind and interesting people I've had the privilege to meet.

Bolstered by Blue Skirt Lady's friendly welcome, we entered Simmons Chapel feeling hopeful. Sure enough, there were pants-wearing ladies all around us. And with the church located within WEEE's viewing area, quite a number of folks recognized me and greeted both of us warmly.

The interior of the church reminded me so much of the church where my paternal grandparents had been members. The walls were heart pine beadboard in a natural finish coated only by a layer of clear varnish, now aged to a yellowish-brown patina. Brass and milk glass lighting hung from long brass chains that rose to the ceiling and ended in beautiful decorative medallions.

Six large stained glass windows were evenly spaced along each side wall, each beautifully depicting a scene from the Bible, from the Garden of Eden to the Empty Tomb. A final window front and center behind the pulpit displayed Jesus' baptism, a glowing Jesus rising from the water and a white dove hovering above Him.

The pulpit was old, maybe even the original, and it also brought me memories of my grandfather. Papa Woodward had built the pulpit at their church, a gorgeous and indestructible mass of oak and cedar. I pulled my mind out of the past and joined in the congregational singing.

One hymn was new to me, "The Servant Song," written by a Richard Gillard. I loved it the moment I heard it, and sang out the last verse with sincere emotion: "Brother, sister, let me serve you; let me be as Christ to you; pray that I may have the grace to let you be my servant too."

After that, a trio of young sisters, who looked like 10-11-12 doorsteps, took the stage, violins in hand. Doubting Millie and equally Doubting Judy nudged each other and prepared for the worst. Instead, our ears were met with a moving rendition of "Amazing Grace" that didn't leave a dry eye in the building. The next congregational number was belted out with gusto, having been fueled by the worshipful sounds we'd just experienced.

As we congregants were once again seated, Reverend Pratt rose from his seat on the left front pew, mounted the stage, and placed his Bible on the pulpit. "Folks, if I can't preach after all that, it's time for y'all to run me off," he said, eliciting laughter from everyone.

"I see a lot of new faces out there," he continued, "and we welcome every one of you. Matter of fact, let me ask y'all to stand up one more time, turn to the people around you, and introduce yourselves. Let's not let anyone leave here without knowing how glad we are to have them."

Order turned to minor chaos as a number of people pushed toward me and Millie. I shook dozens of hands and introduced Millie all around. Three or four minutes later, all voices dropped to mere whispers and everyone was back in their seats.

9

"I see y'all have met our local celebrity," Reverend Pratt said as we all were seated. "Bargainomics Lady—I apologize, but I can't recall your real name," he added, "how about introducing yourself and telling us who you brought with you?"

Millie was used to this by now, but it still put her uncomfortably in the spotlight, albeit momentarily. "I'd be glad to," I said, standing and smiling politely. "My real name, Reverend, is Judy Bates," I began, "and this," I said with a wave of my hand, "is my cousin Millie Caffee. Stand up, Millie," I urged. She begrudgingly did so.

"Millie is not only my cousin, but a very talented artist and my frequent traveling companion," I added. "We're enjoying a few days at the lake and decided to visit Simmons Chapel," I explained. Millie took that as her cue to sit, and I did likewise.

"Well, we're very happy to have y'all with us," Reverend Pratt continued. "Any other visitors who'd like to introduce themselves?"

His eyes moved across the congregation and, seeing no volunteers, he added, "I'm positive I don't recognize some of y'all, and I don't think my memory is failing me yet, so if you are a visitor, we'd appreciate if you'd fill out the form you see inside your order of worship and we'll send you some information about our church.

"And before you panic," he continued, grinning broadly, I promise we won't show up on your doorstep, or put you on a mailing list, or in any other way hound, harass, or hassle you." Another round of chuckles sounded throughout the sanctuary.

"Now," Reverend Pratt said, "I know most, if not all, of you have heard or seen the news about the theft of my truck. Since that time, it seems every repeat of the story gets bigger. I've even heard I got shot," he said, and a gasp went through the audience.

"Thank the Lord, that's not what happened," he quickly added. "It wasn't a pleasant experience, but I wasn't harmed in any way. I'm not going to let this incident make me bitter. I choose to let it make me better. I'm praying for the two that took my truck, and I hope the rest of you will join me."

"I've also heard that the thieves were black," he said to his almost entirely white congregation. Reverend Pratt gave a nod to the one African-American couple in his audience.

"They were not," he said, his voice growing sterner. "Folks, it's so easy to want to blame someone who's different. It's so convenient to be able to say to others, 'Well, it wasn't one of *us*,' he continued.

121

"But *us* at Simmons Chapel is the family of God, period. And my Bible tells me, *There is neither Jew nor Greek, there is neither bond nor free, there is neither male nor female: for ye are all one in Christ Jesus,*" he passionately thundered, quoting Galatians 3:28.

"My Bible also says God doesn't worry so much about the outside, but looks at the heart. Yes, whoever committed that crime might have hearts as black as night, but on the outside, they were as white as me. Or you, Brother Raymond," he said, pointing to a redheaded, freckle-faced gentleman.

"I'm not saying either one of those folks were milk white, but I am saying they definitely weren't black. My point is, though, before I take up all my sermon time with this commercial," he smiled, "is that we don't need to make any issues about color. Ned and Leticia," he said, again indicating the African-American man and woman, "we love y'all. I believe you know that, but I just want to get those words on public record."

A round of applause followed his statement and every person within reach of Ned and Leticia patted a shoulder or echoed the reverend. He put up a hand to call for silence. "Before y'all starting slipping out the back to get to Frankie's, I better get on with my sermon. Brother Raymond, how about you lead us in a moment of prayer before I introduce my topic."

The lanky redhead stood and lifted up a prayer that my spirit fully agreed with. "Amen," we all said in unison. Brother Raymond reclaimed his seat and Reverend Pratt cleared his throat and opened his Bible.

"Please turn with me to the book of Matthew," he instructed.

The reverend's sermon was a simple message about God's grace. By the end of the service, I'd made a number of notes on my order of service and, in my Bible, had underlined several passages of scripture he had included.

So many people took the time to meet us and chat that the church was almost empty by the time we made it to the doorway. Reverend Pratt still stood, shaking the hands of the grownups and patting the heads of the children who were the last few to file out and proceed toward Sunday dinner.

For any non-Southerners, an explanation of the terms *dinner* and *supper* is in order. *Dinner* and *supper* are somewhat interchangeable, but not exactly. *Supper* is always the evening meal of the day, while *dinner* could refer to the midday meal or the evening one. It mostly depends on how serious the eating is.

Sundays, being feast days for most families, the midday meal served after a church service is rarely called *lunch*. It's *Sunday dinner*, and, whether eaten at a restaurant or in a home, it typically consists of a passel of friends and kinfolk, and a smorgasbord of meats, vegetables, breads, desserts, and *fixin's*—those extras like homemade relish, pepper sauce, and such.

Buffets are big in the South, and without some gastronomic discipline, so are the people. We Southerners love our food, and almost every denomination claims to have the world's finest fried chicken cook among their members.

123

When we finally made it to Reverend Pratt, he shook both our hands and called to an attractive ash blonde gathering left-behind orders of service, "Honey, I'll take care of that later. Come over here and meet Judy and Millie."

The woman stopped her task and came over. "So nice to meet you both," she said. "I'm Trish, and I'm a fan," she smiled. "Sounds like Bargainomics Anonymous."

We all laughed.

"And Victor appreciates that I take your tips to heart," Trish continued. "My outfit," she said, turning in a slow circle to give us a full view of the lavender capris, matching jacket, and multi-colored print top she was wearing, "cost a total of sixteen dollars," she said.

"Beautiful," I said, and Millie nodded agreement.

"The jacket and pants came from Divine Consigns—eight-fifty."

"We were there yesterday," Millie told her.

"One dollar for the top. At a yard sale," Trish went on. "Shoes from Goodwill—three-fifty," indicating her adorable strappy white sandals. "And finally, my necklace, earrings, and bracelet—three for the set at the Salvation Army." The earrings were small gold and white doorknockers and the matching chain bracelet and necklace alternated links of white and gold.

"You do yourself proud," I said.

"And your husband," Millie added. "Maybe you should show up and model at Judy's next speaking engagement."

"Better yet, I need to check our church calendar and get you to come here to teach some Bargainomics," Trish said. "And Victor's tie was another bargain from Divine Consigns—a Michael Kors for five dollars."

"I hate to interrupt, ladies," Reverend Pratt said, "but I'm as hungry as a bear. Millie and Judy, if y'all don't have any lunch plans, we'd love to have you join us for Sunday dinner." As I said, in the South, calling a meal *lunch* and *dinner* in the same breath made perfect sense.

"We don't want to impose," I said.

"Nonsense," Reverend Pratt said. "And how about y'all dispense with the 'Reverend' thing and just call me Victor."

"Victor it is," I said, "and we'd be honored to share Sunday dinner with you two."

"If y'all want to follow us in your car," Trish said, "we're going to Frankie's. Are y'all familiar with it?"

"No," Millie said. "We figured Frankie must be the best cook among your members," she teased.

Victor and Trish got a laugh out of that. "Frankie's is an all-you-can-eat buffet out on 157," Victor explained. "If you can't find something you like at Frankie's, there's something wrong with you."

"My problem," I said, "is knowing when to stop, not finding what I like. About the only thing you can put in front of me that I won't eat is gefilte fish," I said, referring to a dish made from deboned ground fish. "Other than that, I'm game for anything."

"Me too," said Millie, "but I'd like to add haggis to that list." She and I had given it a try at a Scottish heritage festival. Larry and Bill had wisely declined to sample it.

"I agree," I said. "I didn't think of that one."

"I've heard of haggis, but I have no idea what it is," said Trish.

"You'll be sorry you asked," I told her. "It's a sort of pudding made from the heart and lungs and other yucky parts of a sheep. You chop that up and mix it with onion, oatmeal, and a few other things ..."

"I'm sorry already," Trish said.

"Oh, but here's the best part," I told her. "Then you stuff all that into the sheep's stomach—saved just for this special occasion—tie it up, and boil it. Now how tasty does that sound?"

"I'm officially putting haggis on my things-I'll-never-eat list," Trish told us. "I promise there's no gefilte fish or haggis at Frankie's."

"But you can try some frog legs," Victor added. "The Sunday buffet includes them in with the seafood."

"My list just grew another item longer," I said.

"Preacher," a man hollered from the line at the salad bar, "we'd done given up on you coming. I see you brought that bargain woman and her cousin with you. Bargain Lady, can you get us all a discount on our dinner?"

If only he knew how many times I'd heard that one. "If I'd known ahead of time, I probably could have," I called back.

Half the church was at Frankie's and several members waved at me and Millie as we found a place in the line for the main dishes. Millie and I were experienced buffet diners. We wanted to at least taste everything we possibly could, so wasting stomach space on salad was out of the question.

When we'd mounded our plates to the maximum, we looked around for an open table. Brother Raymond, Ned and Leticia, and five other people were seated at one long table. Leticia waved and motioned for us to join them. "We can slide one more table over," she said. "That'll make room for the four of you."

The group had already made some serious headway on their plates, so one of the men, who later introduced himself as Cecil, said for Victor's benefit, "We've done asked the blessing, Reverend, but you're welcome to do it again. Especially," he chuckled, "if you'll pray for all these calories not to stick with me." He patted his more than ample belly.

"Cecil," Victor said, "don't you know Sunday calories don't count?"

"I knew there was a reason we kept him around," Cecil chortled. And the entire table joined in.

Several people—Simmons Chapel folks and other diners— stopped by to say hello to me and to speak to the pastor and his wife. In between all that, Millie and I ate enough food to satisfy a pair of lumberjacks, while keeping up a lively conversation with everybody at our table. We'd yet to even sample a dessert.

When the ones who'd beaten us to the trough rose to leave, we hugged and goodbyed as if we'd known each other forever. If Larry and I were ever at the lake on a Sunday, we'd definitely be driving around to Simmons Chapel. These were our kind of people.

Finally, only me, Millie, Victor, and Trish were left at our table. "This has been a wonderful day," I said. "The music, your sermon, the people, the food. It's all been great."

"I second that," Millie said.

"They're a fine bunch of folks," Victor said.

"Salt of the earth," Trish added.

"I know you've been asked about the carjacking until you're sick of talking about it," Millie said, "but would it be okay if we asked you a few questions?"

"I don't see why not," Victor said. "As long as you don't shove a camera or microphone in my face," he joked.

"Scout's honor," Millie said, holding up her hand in what she hoped was the Girl Scout salute.

"First," I said, "we need to tell you that we've seen your truck."

"You what!" Victor and Trish said in unison.

"You do mean since it's been stolen?" Victor asked.

"Right," I said. "Have the police said anything about it?"

"Not a peep," Victor said. "How, where, and when did you see it?"

"We'd seen the news report," I said, "so when a truck fitting that description passed right by us yesterday morning, we were pretty sure it was yours." I went through the entire story of our Saturday adventure, ending with our making a report at the Sheriff's Department.

"I don't know whether to call you brave or crazy," Trish said to Millie after hearing about the photos she'd taken.

"That's what I said. Let's have some dessert and coffee and we can talk some more," I suggested. "Unless you two are in a hurry."

"We're in no rush at all," Victor assured us. "We just need to have time for a power nap before this evening's service, which y'all are welcome to come back for."

"Thanks," I said, "but we'll probably stay put once we get back to our friend's lake house." I explained about our arrangement with Jane.

"That's a pretty sweet deal," Victor said.

"She's a very sweet lady," I responded. "And speaking of sweets …" We all made a beeline for the desserts.

Our waitress had already left four cups of coffee on our table, so we plunked down our plates and dug in. I spent a few seconds opening creamer containers and stirring in a pack of stevia.

"I see you like a little coffee with your creamer," Victor said.

Yeah, that's another one I hear a lot. "Only a smidgeon," I said. "Wouldn't want to ruin the taste of all this creamer."

I'd piled on a sample of every dessert I could fit on one plate and I'd still had to pass up a half dozen offerings. Millie had a similarly laden plate in front of her.

As I've already explained, Millie is not into sharing. Oh, she'd give you the shirt off her back, but you'd better keep your fingers and fork to yourself. Nobody, Bill included, was allowed to eat off her plate. I, on the other hand, am notorious for stabbing samples from other people's food, but I'm just as free with offering samples from my own.

Which brings me back to the seafood platter at Lulu's I had mentioned. When normal people choose to share the seafood platter—Sammie and I, for example—the waitress brings out the platter full of seafood, a bowl of slaw, and an empty extra platter. Then Sammie and I, or any other normal person, sits there and divides the full platter, putting half on the empty platter and, daring souls that we are, raking half the slaw from the bowl directly onto the extra platter.

When Millie's with me and we order the seafood platter, I believe the waitress goes back to the kitchen and announces, "Shared seafood platter for the weirdo." Then back in the safety of the kitchen where Millie can't see it happen, these folks graciously go ahead and plate the food onto two platters and halve a serving of slaw between two bowls. I can't explain her, but I love her.

So here we sat, with two plates of dessert samples, either of which would be enough for both of us. But, when it came to food in any shape or fashion, Millie's theme song was "I Shall Not Be Moved," and she was sticking to it.

About that time, Trish looked at our plates and said, "Ooh, that chocolate lava looks delicious. Victor and I completely overlooked it. May I?" She extended a spotlessly clean, unused spoon toward Millie's plate.

"Here," I said, lifting my plate to block Trish's access to Millie's. "Try some of mine."

"Oh, thank you," Trish said, dipping out a tiny bite and savoring it. "Mmmmm," she sighed. "I may have to go back and get a little of that."

"You're most welcome," I said, nudging Millie's foot beneath the table. "It's always nice to share." Zing! One arrow fired into the heart of the selfish one. Who flatly ignored me.

"It sure is," Victor agreed. "If we ever go out for breakfast, Trish and I love to split the big breakfasts with pancakes, eggs, sausage, and everything. It gives us both plenty of good food and saves us money."

"And keeps us both from overeating," Trish added. "Which is why Frankie's is strictly a Sunday treat. And not even every Sunday."

"Larry and I do that too," I said. "But I also like to try different foods, so we sometimes order two entirely different plates and divide what's on them." Ka-pow! Another thing Millie wouldn't even consider.

By now, Millie was eating in silence while the other three of us carried the conversation. "Are you enjoying your desserts?" I asked ever so sweetly.

"Every crumb of them," Millie answered, shoveling in a chunk of cheesecake.

I hoped I wasn't consigned to the other bedroom tonight. I'd make iced coffees this evening. That should help soothe her ruffled feathers.

"So you never got a look at who was in it?" Victor asked, going back to the topic of his pickup.

"No," Millie said, swallowing her cheesecake. "By the time I snapped two photos, he or she had spotted me and took off."

"I'm pretty sure it was a man," I said. "When the truck passed us earlier that morning, I'm almost positive it was a man I saw driving."

"Nobody else was in there?" Trish asked.

"No," I answered. "Only the driver."

"Of course, the person in the truck behind Seafood King might not have been the same person that passed us on the roadway," Millie pointed out. "There was a good bit of time between those two sightings. The first guy could have handed off the truck to someone else. Maybe the guy who helped him steal it."

"Certainly possible," Trish agreed.

"Victor," I said, "I know you've been asked this over and over, but was there anything about either of those guys that you haven't already mentioned? Something you might not have remembered before?"

"Like what?" he said.

"Well, let's take these two criminals one at a time," I said.

132

Spotting our waitress looking in our direction, I hand-signaled a request for another round of coffee. She nodded and scurried off toward the back, returning shortly with a carafe of coffee and a bowlful of creamers.

"I'll leave these with y'all," she said, depositing the carafe and creamers on the table.

"Thank you," we said, and she darted off to take care of other customers.

My daddy has always said that the majority of waiters and waitresses are some of the hardest working, least appreciated, underpaid people on the planet. Even though we'd served ourselves at the buffet, our waitress had kept our empty plates cleared, our glasses and cups full, and had been as cheerful as could be as she went about it. I planned to leave a generous tip for her service.

"The smaller guy," I said, "was wearing a duster. Awfully hot weather for a get-up like that. Was it possible it was to disguise the fact that he was a she?"

Victor thought about this for a minute, closing his eyes and considering my question. "Very possible," he finally said. "Small hands. He or she had small hands."

"Okay," I said, "now compare those to the bigger guy's. What else was different about them?"

Victor again shut his eyes, frowning in deep concentration. A minute ticked by. Millie, Trish, and I waited in silence.

"The ring," he said. "That big guy was wearing an orange

ring."

"What kind of ring?" I asked.

"A band," he said. "Like a wedding band. But orange. Orange as can be. Wow!" he said. "I can see it clear as a bell now."

"Fantastic!" I said. "Anything else you can remember about it?"

"It wasn't plastic," he said. "It was simple, but manly-looking. And not cheap."

"Like this?" Millie asked, having done a quick search for "orange titanium ring" on her cell phone. She handed Victor her phone, and Trish leaned in to look with him.

Victor studied the screen a few seconds, then scrolled down a few times before stopping. "That's it," he said, touching the screen and enlarging one particular photo. "At least, it was very, very similar."

Victor turned the phone so Millie and I could see. It was an orange titanium band with the narrowest of silver edges at both the top and bottom.

"This'll be a big help to the police," I told him. "Did the investigating officer leave you his card?"

"He did," Victor replied, leaning to one side to extract his wallet from his hip pocket. "I've got it right here somewhere," he said, pulling out a stack of cards and sorting through them. "Here," he said, sliding me a plain white card displaying the Winston County Sheriff's Department logo.

"You want me to send him this photo?" Millie asked. "I'll

explain that you're the one that identified it."

"That'd be great," Victor said. "I'm not too up on all this tech stuff."

Millie's fingers flew across the tiny screen and, moments later, she set her phone down and announced, "Done."

10

As we stood to take our leave, Victor's phone came to life with the chorus of "I'll Fly Away." "Excuse me," Victor said to all of us. Then, turning to Trish, he quickly added, "Hon, will you take care of the bill while I take this?" Trish nodded and Victor hurried toward the exit.

"I can't tell you what a pleasure this has been," Trish said. "You've both been so kind and so helpful. Victor and I want to treat you to lunch today."

"Oh, the pleasure's all ours," I insisted. "And we'd like to pay for your meals instead."

"I can't let you do that," Trish responded.

This was typical. Where some folks fought over who had to pay the bill, Millie and I had been taught the importance of generosity and sharing our blessings. Obviously, so had Trish and Victor.

"Look," Millie said, "we know y'all are out a pickup truck, not that we've given up on it being found. But y'all have been through a trauma. The least we can do to help is pay for two Sunday dinners."

"Well, thank you," Trish said. "We really appreciate it."

"First thing, though," I said, "is a trip to the little girls' room." After three glasses of tea and two cups of coffee, I was amazed I'd been able to hold out as long as I had.

Speaking of restrooms, here's a subject that's always fascinated my husband. It cracks Larry up for one woman to get up from the table and invite the other ladies to join her in a trip to the facilities. "Y'all want to run to the restroom before we leave?"

We were discussing this one day when Larry said, "You don't hear me going, 'Bill, you want to go with me to the men's room?' If I said that, Bill would think I was some kind of weirdo. Men don't invite other men to go to the toilet."

"Maybe not in words," I'd countered, "but y'all do it just the same. We walk into a restaurant and you say, 'I'm going to go wash my hands.' Bill may not say a word, but off he goes to the same restroom. Women are simply more verbal about it."

As Trish and I stood at the sinks checking our hair and reapplying lip gloss, Millie called from one of the stalls, "You might know it. I always pick the one that's out of paper. Can one of y'all roll some off and pass it to me under the door?"

Before Trish or I could answer, another woman's voice responded. "Here you go, hon. And if you need any more, just holler. I may be here a few minutes."

"Thanks," came Millie's reply.

137

I love being a Southerner.

We found Victor standing beside their borrowed transportation, motor running. "Thought I'd get the A/C going," he said. "If I'd had your keys, I'd have done the same for y'all."

"Who was on the phone, Victor?" Trish asked, a hint of concern in her voice. "Is everything all right?"

"Everything's fine," he assured her. "That was the deputy investigating the carjacking," Victor said. "He was verifying the information you sent him," he explained, looking at Millie.

"Smart," I said. "Sad but true, they probably get false information fairly often. Good thing he checked with you before he chased a rabbit trail."

"If I'm not getting too nosy, is there anything else wrong?" I asked. "You seemed a little jumpy when Victor got that phone call."

Trish looked embarrassed, but smiled as she said, "Victor says I'm transparent. My mom lives with us," she explained. "She has dementia. Sometimes we're able to bring her to church, but this wasn't one of her good days."

"But she's still able to stay by herself for a few hours?" I asked.

"Oh, no," Trish hurriedly replied. "I wouldn't leave Mom unsupervised for 15 minutes. The stories I could tell you! We're so blessed to have an entire list of volunteers from the church who take turns sitting with her whenever I need a break or Victor isn't available to help me. Brother Raymond's wife Doris is with her today. Bless her heart, she told us not to be in any rush to get back. It's a rare treat to get to stay out like this."

"How wonderful to have so much help you can depend on," Millie said. "Most people aren't that fortunate."

"That's so true," Trish said. "Before Mom's condition got this bad, I was a home health nurse. I saw so many people who had no help from family or friends. My profession's another blessing— being able to do so much of Mom's care myself."

"But you aren't working any now, are you?" I asked.

"No," Trish said. "Mom is my full-time job."

Which explains the truck having been their only transportation. Trish's income was probably their bigger paycheck. What a sacrifice she'd made to care for her mother. Her next statement made me suspect she'd heard what I was thinking.

"We've had to give up a few things for me to be able to stay with Mom," Trish said, "but I dare anyone to call that 'sacrifice.' I would do anything for my mother. And so would Victor," she added, reaching over and squeezing Victor's hand. "And I know, if the situation was reversed, Mom would do the very same for me."

At that point, I think we all got a bit misty-eyed. Suddenly Millie let out a gasp.

"What is it?" I asked.

"The bill!" she yelped. "None of us paid for our dinners!"

"Good grief!" I exclaimed. Then, turning to Victor and Trish, I added, "Y'all don't have to wait on us. Go on home and we'll take care of this and make our apologies."

"But ..." Victor began.

"We've already lost that fight, honey," Trish said. "Judy and Millie insisted on paying."

"First, though, put your cell phone numbers into my phone," I said, handing her mine. "I'll send your info to Millie."

That done, we shared final hugs, then dashed for the register. "We're so sorry," I said, when we finally reached the front of the line. "We went outside and were talking, and realized we'd forgotten to pay for our dinners. I need to pay for four." Millie could reimburse me her half later.

"You're that TV lady, aren't you?" the cashier said.

"Guilty as charged," I said, smiling.

"The tickets for you and that lady with you, and the preacher and his wife have all been paid," she said.

"By who?" I asked, even if *whom* was more proper. Even the grammar police need a day off every now and then.

"An anonymous party," she said, "who swore me to secrecy and threatened bodily harm to myself and my entire family if I told you who did it."

"Well, I wouldn't want to cause all that trouble," I said, "but whoever it was, we sure do appreciate their kindness."

We started out the door and our waitress, who had been generously tipped by all of us before we left the table, ran to catch us. "I never was any good at secrets," she said. "Ned and Leticia did it. Y'all enjoy the rest of your Sunday."

"Now, wasn't that sweet?" I said. "And if you hadn't heard all that, I could still bill you for your half of the dinners," I told Millie.

"Funny," Millie deadpanned. "Shoot Trish a text and tell on them."

"Doing that right now," I said, stepping to one side so as not to block the doorway.

Seconds later, Trish's text arrived. "No surprise there. Those two are good people."

Back at the lake house, we decided our first order of business was a swim. Most of the weekenders were gone and the water was as smooth as glass. This was the ultimate time of day to water ski. Unfortunately, Millie had never pulled anyone on skis, and I wasn't big on the idea of being her guinea pig.

Towels in hand, we padded down to the boathouse. As we came down the stairs and glanced toward the fishing and pontoon boats, Millie grabbed my arm in a panic.

"What's the matter?" I asked.

"There's a body in the boat," she said, lowering her voice and pointing toward the pontoon.

"Get real," I said, stepping around her to see for myself.

She was right. On the floor of the pontoon was a body. A male body, wearing shorts and a t-shirt, and crumpled into an unnatural heap.

"Don't panic," I said. "Wait here." I stepped onto the pontoon. The boat gently rocked, but the body didn't budge.

I made as wide a swath as possible around it, hoping to preserve whatever evidence there was. Leaning down, I could see it was a young man, probably in his late teens. His eyes were closed. His mouth was open and there was the tiniest hint of saliva on his bottom lip. The body, it seemed, was also softly snoring.

Holding a finger to my lips, I signaled for silence, then put my palms together and leaned my head to one side, placing one palm against my cheek. The international sign for sleeping. If it wasn't, it should be. Then I pointed to the fishing boat and made a rowing motion. I was getting pretty good at this.

Millie gave me a thumbs-up and retrieved the wooden paddle. When she handed it across to me, I backed away from Rip Van Winkle and gently nudged his foot with the end of the paddle. Rip elicited a snort and rolled over.

This time, I was pulling no punches. I eased around to the steering console and reached into the pocket beside the gear shift. Waving the object so Millie could see it, I forewarned her to cover her ears before I let lose a blast of the air horn.

Our young stowaway came to life, so terrified that he almost went from prone to standing in a single leap. "Wha-what's that?" he yelled. "Whatta you think you're doing?"

"A better question is what do *you* think you're doing?" I yelled back, wielding the boat paddle once again. My ears were still ringing from the air horn.

142

"Who are you?" he demanded.

"We'll ask the questions, Mister," Millie chimed in, now armed with a folded camp stool.

"My name's Hadley," he said. "Hadley Vincent." And you can put that paddle down, okay?" he said, looking at me. "And the stool too," he said, turning toward Millie.

"Why should we?" I said. Neither of us dropped our weapons.

"Didn't Mrs. Adderly tell you about me?" he asked.

He knew Jane. Or at least, he knew her name. "How do you know her?" I asked, hanging onto my paddle.

"I'm her yard man," he said.

"Young man," Millie said, "finding a complete stranger sleeping in a boat that doesn't belong to him is highly suspicious. Therefore," she said, punctuating her statement with a forward thrust of her camp stool, "expecting us to believe you're here to do yard work is equally suspect." She pointed to the unmowed lawn.

"And where, pray tell, is your vehicle?" I asked. "How did you get here? And where is your mower and other equipment? Talk fast, or I'm calling the police," I warned, shifting the paddle to one hand and using my other to yank my cell phone from my shorts pocket.

"I walked," he said. "Mrs. Adderly has her own equipment in the shed on the side of the house opposite the driveway. Have you ladies even walked around this place?" he asked as if we were to blame for not understanding.

"You walked, huh?" Millie said, still unconvinced. "From

143

where?"

"Actually, on this particular occasion, I hitchhiked to the turnout and walked from there."

"All right, Mr. Hadley," I said, "show us some identification."

"And no sudden moves," Millie added.

"Just don't hit me, okay?" he pled. "I'm going to reach in my back pocket." He lifted out a black nylon wallet and extracted a driver's license. "Here," he said, holding it out toward Millie and her camp stool.

Millie stepped up as close as she dared and studied the license. "It's him, all right," she said. "Now what?"

Reluctantly, I lowered my paddle. "March yourself up to the house. You've still got some explaining to do."

We ordered Hadley to take a seat on the porch. While Millie kept an eye on him, I went in the house and made three glasses of lemonade. Hadley had asked us to call him "Hat" and had pulled a folded baseball cap out of the back of his waistband and jammed it on his head by way of explanation.

"Okay, Hat," Millie said. "How does a transportation-less, mower-less fellow like yourself end up working for Mrs. Adderly?"

"Actually, I have my own mower," Hat said, "but it's kinda hard to get it here without a set of wheels."

"And how does a wheel-less person do yard work?"

"Look," he said, "I have my own wheels too, but the transmission in my truck went out a couple weeks ago. Before that,

I'd been driving over here. And hauling my own equipment," he added.

"So Jane, uh, Mrs. Adderly knows about your wheel-less situation?" I asked.

"Not exactly," Hat said, taking a big gulp of lemonade and fidgeting badly. Either he needed a bathroom or he was lying through his teeth. Or both. At least that was my experience when my and Millie's kids were youngsters.

"Would you like to use the restroom?" I asked.

"Would I ever!" exclaimed Hat, jumping to his feet almost as quickly as when I'd used the air horn. Without hesitation, he darted through the French door, into the kitchen, and around to the bathroom off the guest bedroom. Clearly he'd been here before.

I stepped inside and waited, making sure he wasn't taking this opportunity to rummage through my personal items I'd left in that bathroom. If he'd done more than glance, it'd had to have been at record speed. I heard a flush and then the sound of water running in the sink. That was, at least, a sign of good hygiene.

When I escorted him back to the porch, Millie was standing, hands on hips. "Sit back down, Hat," Millie ordered. "A new question has suddenly popped into my mind."

"Okay," he said. "But first, y'all don't have anything a fella could eat, do you?"

For Pete's sake! We were ready to call the police on this guy a few minutes ago. Since then, he'd been promoted to drinking our lemonade and using our bathroom. And now he wanted us to fix him a meal? Millie and I would have made terrible prison guards. It'd have been like Aunt Bea with Otis on *Andy Griffith.* "Here, Hat. Would you like another slice of our homemade apple pie? How about a nice cold glass of milk to wash it down?"

"We do," Millie said. "Seafood salad, pizza, pineapple ..."

"Pizza'll be great," Hat said, already rising and heading toward the kitchen.

"After you." Millie's voice dripped with sarcasm. Wasted on Hat.

I gave Millie a shrug that said, "I don't get it," and she mouthed back to me, "Follow my lead."

Hat stood at the island, gazing longingly at a bag of potato chips. "Is it all right if I chow down on a few of these chips while I wait on the pizza?" he asked.

"The pizza's already cooked," Millie said. "You'll just need to warm it in the microwave."

"Cold pizza's fine with me," Hat said.

"Oh, but it'll be even better once it's warmed," Millie insisted, giving me a look that left me utterly clueless. "You grab a paper plate while I snag the pizza from the fridge."

"Cool," Hat said. He shuffled to the pantry door, opened it, and took out a paper plate. You ladies gonna be joining me?"

"Aha!" Millie said, waving the plastic bag of leftover pizza.

"Huh?" said Hat.

"Huh?" said I.

"How did you know where to find the paper plates, Hat?"

146

Millie questioned.

"Uh, the pantry," he said. "Pretty logical."

"Wrong," Millie said. "That could have been a broom closet for all you'd know. Look around at all these cabinets," she continued, using her best Vanna White wave. "The only way you could have possibly gone straight to those plates was ..."—she paused and I knew she was totally in character as the great Poirot—"... if you had already been here before!" Her eyes danced with triumph as she made her pronouncement.

"That's right!" I said. "Okay, Hat, cut the baloney. Have you or haven't you been in here?"

"Yeah, okay, you got me," Hat said. "But it was only for a few nights."

Millie and I both arched an eyebrow and glared at Hat without speaking.

"Okay, okay," Hat said, folding. "A couple weeks. There, I said it. But, man, I was desperate."

"You're the one who tried to break into my bedroom Thursday night!" I shrieked.

"Guilty," said Hat. "Hey, I'm sorry.

11

"Technically," Hat said as he slid several slices of pizza onto a plate and expertly programmed the microwave, "it was my room before it was yours."

To which I said, "So you're the one who'd been sleeping in my bed." It was the story of the three bears, with pizza rather than porridge. "And you're also the one who left those dirty towels and washcloths in the bathroom floor."

The microwave beeped and Hat opened the door, stuck one finger to a slice of pizza, and pronounced it, "El perfecto."

"I don't mean to be rude," Hat said through a mouthful of pizza, "but it wasn't your bed. And I had every intention of throwing those towels in the washer, had my accommodations not been unexpectedly taken over. And gimme a little credit. I didn't even run the A/C—just the ceiling fan."

"Are you saying Mrs. Adderly didn't tell you we were coming to stay here?" Millie asked.

"Uh, no," Hat said, like we were the two dumbest people on

the planet. "I'm her yard man, not her confidante. I take care of the lawn. I let her know when I'm coming to do the work, and she leaves me her payment."

"Where?" asked Millie. "On your pillow in your bedroom?"

"No need for the sarcasm," Hat said. "She leaves it in an envelope inside the grill."

"And how does that entitle you to break into her home and treat it as if it were your own?" I asked.

"Funny you should put it that way," Hat chuckled, "because, actually, it kinda is."

"What's that supposed to mean?" Millie snapped. "First you were a breaker and enterer. Now you're the home owner."

"I never broke anything," Hat pointed out. "I only entered."

"And what does any of that have to do with you being the home owner?" I persisted.

"Aw, I was just messing with you," Hat said. "Got any dessert around here?"

While the brownies were in the oven, we adjourned to the living room where Millie and I took our usual seats on the sofa and Hat flopped into one of the chairs. "You're not cutting grass today," I said. "After we have some brownies, we'll drive you home."

"That could be a problem," he said.

"And just what's that supposed to mean?" Millie asked.

"I can't go home," he said. "My parents think I'm in school."

"How old are you?" I asked.

"Nineteen," he answered.

"And what school are you supposed to be in?" The word *reform* crossed my mind. Did they still have those?

"Uh, like college," Hat said. "I'm a sophomore at Grantham U. Go Geckos." He smiled, but the effort was half-hearted.

"So why aren't you there?" Millie asked. "Don't fall classes start right after Labor Day? You should be getting settled in by now."

"It's a little matter of wheels," he said, "and a bigger matter of tuition money."

The timer buzzed and I got up to check the brownies. "More lemonade or would you prefer milk for this round?" I asked.

"Milk," Hat and Millie said. My vote made it unanimous.

So," I said, sliding several brownies onto Hat's pizza plate, "start at the beginning and give us every detail of why you aren't at Grantham and why your parents think you are."

"Okay," he said. "Awesome brownies." He gave a thumbs-up and chugged a third of his milk before continuing. "I hope you don't have any other plans for this evening, because this is gonna be a really long story," he told us.

"My parents used to own a construction company. Mom ran the office and Dad oversaw the job sites. The company made some serious coin, and by the time I was in kindergarten, my family was pretty much rolling in it. That's when Dad built this house."

"So it really was your house!" Millie said. "Or, at least, it used to be."

150

"Right," Hat said. "We didn't live here, though. It was just our lake house, same as the way the Adderlys use it. Our other house was about 70 miles from here, over on the other side of Fall Creek in Greer Station."

Millie and I glanced at each other knowingly. Greer Station was loaded with mansions. We'd even been to one of their Christmas candlelight tours.

"Anyhow, the company won the bid for this colossal bridge project, so Dad hired a guy to help him oversee the project. Turns out this guy was cheating our company left and right. He was taking kickbacks, billing for better materials than he was actually buying. Really bad stuff. When my mom asked Dad about several invoices she'd seen come through the office, he started quietly looking into this guy. Then one day, Dad went out to one of the job sites to have it out with this ..."

"Guy," I finished. "Would he happen to have been named Earl Yarborough?" I asked.

"Yeah, but how'd you know?" Hat asked me.

"I remember when it all happened," I said.

"So do I," Millie echoed. "His name was all over the news. Go ahead, Hat. Finish your story."

"Dad gets there and asks one of the men where Yarborough was. He points to the hill above the retaining wall they were building. So Dad was going up there to have it out with him. Anyhow," Hat continued, "there were several pieces of big machinery up top and a bunch of men working on the wall below.

While Dad was down there speaking to some of the men, the dozer operator lost control, and this gigantic machine went crashing down the hill and hit the retaining wall. A huge section collapsed, penning six of the men underneath. My dad was almost clear of it, but a chunk that broke off landed right on top of him." His voice trembled as he finished his sentence.

"Hat, you don't have to talk about this if you don't want to," I said.

"No, it's all right," he assured me. "It's all part of my story, and you have to know that part to understand the rest of it." With that, he continued.

"When they got all the men out, four were dead and two had what the news media kept calling 'life-threatening injuries.' For my dad, those injuries included two crushed legs, a skull fracture, and a broken back. The other guy who made it was at the other end of the collapse and, like Dad, got hit by a piece that broke off the main collapse. He had a lot of broken bones, but only ended up losing a foot. I say 'only' because, compared to my dad, he was really lucky."

"I remember seeing your dad on the news," Millie said. "That court case really put him through it, and he was already in so much pain—physically and emotionally," she added.

"Yeah, the docs had to amputate Dad's legs, and the head injury turned out to be even worse. He had a lot of memory problems. Still does. But those attorneys badgered and badgered him. Even accused him of faking his head problems."

"And you were only a little boy," I said sympathetically.

"Eight when it happened. Twelve when all the trials were finally finished."

"Your dad was blamed for all those men's deaths," Millie said, "and all their families filed lawsuits against your parents' company."

"And against my parents' personal estate too," said Hat. "I don't understand all of that, but Mom always says the company wasn't 'set up right,' whatever that means."

"So your dad lost everything," I said, recalling the months and months of media coverage during the court case.

"Pretty much. And Yarborough blamed all the crooked stuff on Dad. He swore in court that every inferior product he bought was under the direct orders of my father."

"The inferior materials were found to be the fault of the accident, weren't they?" I asked.

"That's right," Hat said. "Several structural engineers testified that, even with the dozer hitting the wall, the wall would never have collapsed had the proper materials been used."

"But only Yarborough went to prison," Millie said.

"Thanks to Mom's careful recordkeeping," Hat said. "Unlike crooks who keep two sets of records—one with the real info and one that's been doctored—my mom kept two sets of identical records. She kept one on a personal computer at home that wasn't linked to the computers used at the office or job sites."

"So even after Yarborough had falsified the company's

records on the office computer, your mom was able to produce the original documentation."

"Exactly," said Hat. "And the computer forensics examiners proved that the stuff on Mom's computer hadn't been tampered with. But the stuff Yarborough had presented as evidence of my dad's involvement had all been altered, if not downright faked.

Dad stayed out of prison and was found 'not guilty' of the charges related to the inferior materials. But he still had to pay huge settlements to the families of the men who were killed and the other man who survived. That wiped us out. The business went belly up. We lost the house, the lake house, everything. Now Dad's on disability, and Mom takes care of him and does some low-paying work-from-home stuff.

"Like what?" I asked.

"Like as a telephone debt collector. If it wasn't so sad, it'd be funny," Hat said. "Mom despises those kinds of calls."

"Who wouldn't?" Millie said.

"And now she's the one making them," Hat added. "Man, you should hear the way some people talk to her. Do they think she enjoys her job? But, hey, she toughs it out because she knows how badly we need the money."

"So where does your family live now?" I asked.

"Public housing," he said. "Fall Creek Village, or as we residents say, the Village. Sounds a lot nicer than it is. Believe me, it's no village. It's more like a war zone. Drugs, gangs, all of that. Fall Creek brags about their low crime rate, but that's because they've got it all corralled into our lovely neighborhood."

Millie and I had heard about Fall Creek Village. It was just as Hat described it. Ninety-nine percent of the time, if Fall Creek made the news about a shooting or drug bust, it had happened in the Village.

"And how does any of this explain why you're not in school and your parents think you are?" Millie asked.

"Okay," Hat said, "my parents tapped out my college fund before I finished high school. They hated doing it, but there really wasn't any choice. I busted my butt to keep my grades up and got a first-year scholarship to Grantham, but even that was only enough money for the first year's tuition.

"A lot of the businesses around there are really good about hiring us students and working our job schedules around our classes. So I got a pretty good job and worked as many hours as I could, but that gave me just enough money to pay the other expenses—books, gas money, ramen noodles.

"I'd worked every job I could find and finally saved enough money to buy another pickup and pay for the first semester of my sophomore year. The one I'd been driving blew an engine, and fixing that was gonna cost mega-bucks. So instead, I bought another old pickup. But wouldn't you know it? The transmission went out in it. And—story of my life here, ladies—there was no money to get it repaired.

"There's this really cornball old TV show I've seen with some old dudes that sing this song about 'If it weren't for bad luck, I'd have no luck at all." Well, that pretty much describes the Vincent family," he said.

"So where's your truck now?" I asked.

"'If it weren't for bad luck,'" Hat sang. "I left it on the side of the highway where it quit on me. It's like a catch-22. I needed money to pay for a tow truck, and I needed my truck to get to my yard work jobs. No truck, no jobs. No jobs, no money.

"I talked to my regulars, and all of them just dumped me when I told them I didn't have a way to bring my own equipment. Only the Adderlys kept me on and said I could use their stuff.

"Anyway, I was finally able to go to the wrecker service and pay for them to tow my truck to Morton's Garage. Mr. Morton said he wouldn't charge me to leave it there until I had the money to pay for the transmission. So the wrecker goes to get my truck and it's gone. How's that for bad luck?"

"How could anybody steal a truck that won't run?" Millie asked.

"That's just it," Hat said. "Nobody stole it. It got impounded. It's over in another wrecker service's impound lot. And they're charging me for towing it and for every day it's there from the time they picked it up off the side of the road."

"That's terrible!" I said.

"Tell me about it," Hat groaned. "There was no way I was going to dump all these problems on my parents, so I just made out like my truck was in the shop, everything was cool, and I was picking it up and headed on down to Grantham."

"And that's when you came here instead?" Millie asked.

Hat nodded his head and swallowed hard, but didn't answer.

"When's your first day of class?" I asked.

"Next Tuesday," he said. "The day after Labor Day."

I stood, pushed an ottoman over in front of Hat's chair, and sat down facing him. "You've been straight with us. Now I'm going to be straight with you. I'd like to smack you in the head for using the Adderlys' house without their permission, but I'd also like to hug the stuffing out of you because your situation absolutely breaks my heart.

"Now here's what's going to happen," I continued. "First thing in the morning, you're going to take care of this yard work. And in the meantime, Millie and I are going to put our heads together and see if we can come up with an idea to help you. Because if I have to put you in my car and drive you there myself, you'll not miss your first day of class next Tuesday."

Before I could decide whether to hug him or whack him, Hat threw himself forward and hugged the stuffing out of me. "I don't know what to say," he croaked, sniffling into my shoulder.

"I say, don't wipe your nose on my t-shirt," I laughed.

Millie to the rescue. She'd yanked a fistful of tissues from the box on the end table and pushed a few into my hand and Hat's. Hat released me and fell into another hug with Millie.

"What are we going to do with this boy?" Millie asked.

"I guess we'll give him his old room back," I said before giving Hat a hard look and adding, "For now. And you," I said,

157

pointing directly at Hadley, "be prepared to confess your crime to the Adderlys."

"Sweet," Hat said.

"Shower," Millie said. "I suspect you might have missed a couple of those lately. Do you have any more clothes stashed around here?"

"A whole duffel full," Hat replied, "out in the shed."

"While you get those," I said, "I'll clear out my things and move them to Millie's room." Now Millie and I would be sharing both bed and bath. Oh, well, it was certainly not for the first time.

While Hat showered in the guest bath, Millie took her shower and I cleaned up what little mess we'd made with the pizza and brownies. Both Millie and Hat reappeared in the living room wearing clean tees and shorts. I followed the dress code once I'd grabbed my own shower.

"How about a movie?" Millie suggested.

"Fine with me," I said.

"Here, Hat," Millie said, tossing him the remote as he sprawled in the recliner. "You pick."

"But we don't do R-rated," I warned. "PGs are our favorites."

"Whoa, it's going to be a wild night tonight," Hat snickered.

He quickly made a selection and the classic action film, *Vanishing Point*, appeared on the screen. When Barry Newman's name rolled across the screen, I yelled, "Pause!" and Hat obliged. "You remember him," I said. "He played *Petrocelli*. The TV series."

"Oh," Millie said. "We used to watch that show every week."

"Never heard of it," said Hat.

"That's because you weren't even born," I said. "Back to the movie."

This time, it was Millie who ordered Hat to pause.

"Now what?" Hat said. "We haven't even made it through the opening credits."

"It's just that I didn't realize he did any acting," Millie said.

"Who?" Hat and I asked.

"Cleavon Little," she answered, pointing to his name frozen on the screen.

"Of course he did," I said. "He played in lots of stuff. Don't you remember him in *Blazing Saddles*, my least favorite film of all time?"

"No, I thought he was the one who headed up that '60s militant group, the Pink Panthers."

Hat sat speechless. He'd just been introduced to what I call 'Millyisms.' No one was more skilled at jumbling information.

I stifled a huge sigh, looked toward Hat, and rolled my eyes. "No, Millie, that was Eldredge Cleaver," I said. "And his Panthers were Black."

"Oh," she said. "Go ahead with the movie, Hat."

Millie had been doing this as long as I could remember. Way back when we were both in our 20s, she'd blurted out her amazement at how gorillas could be trained to handle weaponry. That was the day I explained to her about *guerilla* warfare.

When I opened my eyes, "The End" was rolling across a backdrop of flames and firemen. "Pssst," I said, nudging Millie with my foot.

"What is it?" Millie said, her eyes fluttering open.

"I don't think any of us saw the end of the movie," I said, nodding toward Hat who was totally zonked, one arm dangling from the chair and the remote in the floor beneath his lifeless fingers.

"Should we wake him?" Millie asked.

"Nah, he's a teenager. They can sleep anywhere."

Millie pulled a lightweight throw from a basket at one end of the sofa and gingerly spread it over Hat. He never moved. "We can leave the hall light on," she said. "That way, if he wakes up and wants to go to bed, he can find his way."

12

Monday morning, Millie and I found the living room unoccupied. When I peeked into the front hallway, the door to Hat's room was closed. When I stuck my ear to his door, the rhythmic snoring told me Hat was blissfully asleep.

I shook my head in wonderment as I went toward the kitchen. The terror of my first night here was now sleeping peacefully while Millie and I prepared to make him breakfast. Life makes some funny twists and turns.

Millie took the griddle out onto the porch and set it up while I mixed batter for pancakes. With a teenager to feed, we wanted to have a more substantial breakfast than fruit and muffins. We ended up with a feast: pecan pancakes with real maple syrup, sausage, bacon, cheese omelets, and toast. When we sat down to eat, there was no sign of Hat.

"Should we wake him?" Millie asked.

"Let's let him sleep," I said. "He's had a rough past few days."

"He's had a rough past few years," Millie said. "How awful it

161

must feel to be an uninvited guest in what used to be your own family's lake house."

"Probably not much worse than being the yard man for the family who now owns it," I said. "When our trained catfish leads us to that gold, we're going to get that boy's truck out of impound and buy him a new transmission."

"Agreed," said Millie.

Mondays were my absolute favorite days to be on the lake. Most of the marinas were closed, which meant even fewer boaters were out than on other weekdays. Millie and I had gassed up the pontoon while we were at Rock Ledge Marina, and we figured the tanks on the Sea-Doos still had plenty of fuel. We were all set for a day on the water, whichever mode of transportation we decided on.

"I'd like some more time on the Sea-Doos," Millie said, "but I'd also like to check out that stretch of shoreline where we saw those divers."

"Let's do it," I said. "I'll put away the rest of the breakfast and leave Hat a note."

The ride to where we'd seen the two divers took less than ten minutes, and Millie and I had come prepared. We stepped off our Sea-Doos and onto the shallow rock ledge that led to the shoreline. Carefully holding our watercrafts off the rocks, we each extracted long lengths of rope from the storage beneath our seats.

With one end of the rope tied to the metal loop on the nose of my Sea-Doo, I slogged to shore and tied the other end to a pine sapling at the edge of the water. Millie did the same. Then we waded back in and gently pushed the Sea-Doos out away from the rocks. With the water calm and no boats about, the Sea-Doos would hopefully stay out from the rocks long enough for us to have a quick look around.

"These water shoes were a great idea," Millie said. "I don't think my tender feet could take much barefoot walking."

"Mine either," I said. "You go left and I'll go right. Holler if you see anything."

We'd been scouting for several minutes when I saw it—a narrow trail leading into the forest. "Pssst," I hissed, hoping Millie could hear me.

No answer. I backtracked to our starting point and began following Millie's wet footprints. Unlike the hard flinty rock in some areas of the lake, this whole stretch was entirely sandstone, worn smooth and rounded by the lapping waves and weathered into sandy soil above the water line.

"There you are," I said quietly when I finally caught up with her. "I've found a trail."

We worked our way back along the shoreline, stopping long enough for Millie to retrieve her phone from her Sea-Doo. "We might need this," she said.

We continued around the bend until I pointed out the narrow opening in the tree line.

"Hard enough to see from right here," Millie said. "No one would ever notice it from out on the water."

"Exactly," I said. "Let's see what's up there. We'll only go a little ways," I promised.

Reluctantly, Millie followed me into the path. "Try to stay to the side," I said. "We don't want to mess up any footprints or clues."

"Are you sure this is a good idea?" Millie asked.

"Of course I'm not," I answered. "But we'll be careful." I picked up a sturdy stick to swing in front of me. Spiders loved stringing webs across paths like this. I had no intention of walking into one.

"This is a deer trail," I whispered, using my stick to point out several sets of tracks going toward and coming from the water. "Busy place," I added, noting prints made by raccoons, foxes, and humans.

Millie pointed to a nasty-looking pile of scat containing everything from berries to rabbit fur. "What is that?" she whispered. "Gross."

"Probably coyote poop," I said.

"Coyotes?" she said. "Are we in danger?"

"If we are," I whispered back, "it's from two-legged creatures."

Ahead of us, a twig snapped and we both froze. We waited and heard nothing, so we slowly inched forward. That's when a big buck snorted, darted across in front of us, and disappeared into the forest.

"I can't believe you didn't scream," I said to Millie, grinning at the terror on her face.

"I couldn't," she replied, breathlessly. "I was too scared. What was wrong with that deer? What was all that horrible gunk hanging off its antlers?"

"He's been in velvet—sort of fuzzy fur over his antlers. That's how they look when they first grow back out."

I could see the bewilderment on Millie's face. "They shed their antlers each year and grow new ones, which start out covered in fuzzy stuff. Right now he's rubbing the velvet off, and pretty soon, he'll look normal," I explained. "There's your nature lesson for the day. Now let's move it along and get in and out of here."

In a clearing half a football field ahead of us, we could make out what appeared to be an Army Surplus tent. We inched along, closer and closer. When the only other sounds were squirrels warning of our approach, we crept warily into the campsite.

Around the tent stood all the comforts of a woodland home: fire ring, clothesline, a pair of folding chaise lounges, and a big plastic ice chest. About eight feet above ground level, a mesh bag of packaged food items hung from a tree limb.

"Looks like these folks have been here a while," I said.

"Yeah, and check out the laundry," Millie said, indicating the clothesline strung between two trees. Two very different sized t-shirts hung next to men's swim trunks and a teeny-weeny bikini. Two neoprene wetsuits covered the rest of the clothesline.

"Our divers," I said.

"Gotta be," said Millie.

165

"And they're still staying here, from all indications. No way they'd leave all this stuff behind, would they?" I asked.

"Surely not," Millie concurred. "Which means they could come back and catch us here. We need to leave. Now."

"Right," I said. "First, take a few pics."

As we took our final turn around the campsite, I stooped and poked my trusty stick into the cold ashes of their campfire, moving them around until a small shred of white paper became visible. "What have we here?" I said, lifting out the tiny scrap.

"Looks like it came from an envelope," Millie said as I stood and held up the paper for her to photograph.

"It's part of an address," I said. "Anto," I read. "373 W something, Fall something. It must be Fall Creek."

"So one of the divers—the big guy—is Anton Somebody from Fall Creek," Millie said.

Light bulb! as Gru of the Minion movies would say. "Not Anton," I said. "Antoine. Remember what Cooter said? 'I ain't told nary a soul, cept'n for y'all and my friend Antoine.' And Antoine told him not to tell anyone."

"No wonder," said Millie. "He wanted all the gold for himself."

"And they may very well have found it," I said. "But if they have, they haven't gotten it all up or haven't figured out how to retrieve it. If they had, they'd be long gone from here."

"Which, I repeat," Millie urged, "means they could show up at any second. The sooner we're out of here, the better."

166

We picked up the pace heading back down the trail, reached the water, untied our Sea-Doos, and took off.

"Where are we going and what are we going to do?" Millie yelled.

I released the throttle and glided to a semi-halt so Millie could pull up beside me. "As far as the divers go, there's nothing we can do," I said. "They probably don't have a camping permit for the Bankhead, but that's not exactly a major offense. They're diving, which isn't illegal. And one of them may or may not be the Antoine that Cooter told us about. No law against being named Antoine."

"Right on all accounts," Millie said. "So now what?"

"I say I give you a guided tour of Smith Lake's *Lifestyles of the Rich and Famous*. Follow me."

We gunned our motors and flew toward the main channel, having more fun than Crockett and Tubbs in their cigar boat on *Miami Vice*. Millie and I watched a lot of those reruns.

I slowed to a crawl and Millie pulled up next to me. "This," I said, beginning the grand tour, "is the home of Lionel Bartlett. He, as you know, owns a Fortune 500 company and flits between here, Birmingham, and New York on a regular basis. Notice the nice little helipad over to the left."

The house was a mammoth two-story built of rough-hewn ash gray planks, with a slate roof and a full-length covered porch fronting both levels. A matching walkway led to an adjoining guest house, a mini-version of the main house. A modest little thing, the guest quarters likely had no more than 1,000 square feet on each of its levels.

Near the waterfront, a manmade waterfall cascaded into a zero entry pool. Luscious greenery sprouted from the stones of the waterfall and a flagstone patio surrounded the pool and led to a slate-roofed outdoor kitchen/dining area with the biggest Green Egg money could buy, a giant flat screen TV, and all the accoutrements of luxurious lakeside entertaining.

From there, a walkway sloped gently downhill to a massive swim pier with slide and diving board, quadruple boathouse with hydraulic lifts, and separate mini boathouse with four lifts holding two top-of-the-line Sea-Doos and a pair of what looked like beached great white sharks.

"What are those?" Millie asked, pointing to the sharks.

"Sea Breachers," I said. "Megabuck submersible watercrafts. They make them in dolphin and killer whale designs too, but apparently Mr. Bartlett wanted sharks."

"They'll actually go underwater?" Millie asked.

"Well, yeah," I said, "but only for short stretches. If you look more closely," I said, puttering a bit closer to the shore, you can see there's a glass bubble like a fighter jet canopy over the cockpit."

"I'd love to try one out," Millie said.

"I'm sure the Bartletts are Bargainomics fans. We'll pull in and ask if we can borrow them," I responded.

"Uh-huh," said Millie. "And while you're at it, see if they'll loan us that Ski Nautique."

We laughed and moved on down what we commoners termed "Millionaires' Row." "We can't get in too close," I warned Millie. "We don't want Officer Jackson showing up and giving us a ticket."

We oohed and aahed past at least two dozen houses before hitting another stretch of Bankhead Forest. "When we get past this," I said, tongue-in-cheek, "we're back to the regular folk," which consisted mostly of high six-figure homes the size of the Adderlys'. We sped through the wooded section, then slowed to admire the slightly less opulent houses along the waterfront.

"Do people live here year-round?" Millie asked.

"In some areas, yes," I said, "but a lot are summer homes."

"Is there anywhere near here where we can get something to drink?" Millie asked. "I'm really thirsty, and we didn't even bring our water bottles."

"I could use a drink myself," I said. "And a snack to go with it. Breakfast is still holding up pretty good, though."

"It should be," Millie said. "That was a total pig-out. And I bet Hat's downed the rest of it by now."

"I don't doubt that one bit," I laughed. "With all the yard work he has to do, he'll need the energy. There's a park a little bit farther up. Their concession stand should be open."

We blasted off again, thoroughly enjoying the wind, the speed, the sun, and everything about this glorious day on the water. After another mile or two, I motioned left and we crossed the main body and cruised into a broad offshoot dotted by a few houses, a marina and RV park, and at last, Yellow Leaf Recreation Area.

Pointing out the no-wake buoy, I slowed to a crawl and so did Millie. We steered well clear of the roped-off swim area and scooted the noses of our Sea-Doos onto a stretch of yellow-white sand beach.

"No way!" a voice called from an umbrella-topped beach chair in the edge of the water. "Aren't you the Bargainomics Lady?" Despite my wild and windswept appearance, it was nice to see that Bargainomics fans were, literally, everywhere.

"You got me," I said, jamming my Sea-U-Later cap onto my wild head of hair.

"Can I get my picture with you?" the lady asked. "My friends are never going to believe this!"

"Of course," I said. "Stay there. I'll come to you."

"Let me just grab my phone," she said, pulling herself up and plodding a few steps to her beach bag.

As usual, I'd worn a t-shirt and shorts over my swimsuit, so I didn't mind getting wet. I sat in the water beside her chair and waited for her to join me. "How's this?" I said.

"My friends are going to be so jealous," she said. "Would you," she said, holding out her phone, "mind taking our picture?"

"Not one bit," Millie responded in a surprisingly sincere manner.

"I'm Genevieve, by the way," the woman said. "Genevieve Jones."

"Nice to meet you, Genevieve," I said. "And this is my cousin Millie."

"Hey, Millie," Genevieve said. "It sure must be fun hanging out with the Bargainomics Lady."

"You have no idea," Millie answered. The real Millie was starting to come out. Then, wading out in front of us in the water, she added, "Y'all smile."

Genevieve and I put on our biggest grins and Millie took what turned out to be an adorable picture, even if my only makeup was sunscreen moisturizer. A big pair of sunglasses could cover up a lot, and Genevieve and I had both kept ours on.

"Send me a copy," I said, handing Genevieve back her phone. "I'll post it on my Facebook page."

"I will!" Genevieve said. "And it was so nice to meet you in person. I'll see you on Thursday!"

We waved and walked on toward the concession stand.

"First things first," Millie said, veering off toward the restrooms.

"Unquestionably," I said, following her lead.

It astounds me that people went into outer space before somebody came up with a two-piece swimsuit that actually covers your body. When I think of all the years I spent having to strip naked to go to the bathroom, it's just ridiculous. Today Millie and I were both wearing modest swim dresses that covered the tops of our legs and had matching bottoms underneath. These made taking a potty break so much easier.

We emerged from our stalls, checked ourselves in a full-length mirror, and followed the smell of hot dogs to the concession stand.

"How can we resist?" Millie asked.

"We have to," I said. "I want to fix a really nice dinner tonight for us and Hat. We won't be all that hungry if we eat hot dogs on top of our big breakfast."

"True," Millie said, "It was a momentary weakness. The aroma got to me."

Reaching the front of the short line, I placed my order. "A pack of baby carrots, a pack of ranch dressing, and a bottle of water, please."

"I think I'll join you," Millie said.

A brief walk brought us to a shaded bench facing the water. We nested in, opened our snacks and water, and proceeded to crunch and munch.

"I wish more places sold healthy snacks like this," Millie said. "Sometimes I end up eating junk simply because that's the only thing available."

"I think we all fight that battle," I said. "I normally bring my own snacks, but I totally forgot this morning."

"And before we take off again, don't dare let me forget my sunscreen," I said, glaring with envy at Millie's flawlessly tanned skin.

"Don't be a hater," Millie said. "It's not like I try to tan."

"Just stop," I said. Knowing her tan was effortless didn't help my feelings.

More in empathy than actual need, Millie dabbed on a tad of sunscreen while I sprayed everything but my eyeballs with BullFrog Water Armor. We waved to Genevieve as we glided by, barely touching our throttles until we cleared the no-wake zone.

"And now?" Millie asked.

"Are you tired of riding?" I asked.

"Are you kidding? I never get to do this. You know this lake far better than I do. Lead the way."

We opened up our watercrafts until we were nothing short of flying. Finally, we came to the familiar fork in the channel. Left went back toward Make-Out Cove. Right went toward Jane's. I slowed to idle and waited for Millie to come alongside.

"No way I'm going back to that cove," Millie said, seeing the nose of my Sea-Doo aimed in that direction.

"There's a lot more lake back there," I told her. "We won't go anywhere near Make-Out Cove," I pleaded.

"Uh-uh," Millie replied, folding her arms across her chest for emphasis.

"All right," I admitted, "we will go near it, but not in it. And we'll hurry by."

"Oh, okay," Millie reluctantly agreed.

"I'll even show you the skinny-dipping hole," I said, wiggling my eyebrows.

"And I'm sure you and Larry have been back there many a time," she said. "Don't tell me anything more or I'll never get those images out of my head."

"I've told you before. I do not kiss and tell. Nor do I strip and tell," I teased.

"TMI, TMI," Millie said, jamming her hands over her ears.

"Oh, come on," I said. "There's a great beach back there too. A nice gentle slope with a sandy bottom. We can sit and relax a while, and then take a swim."

"Would that be Bare Beach?" Millie asked.

"I've never heard a name for it, but next time Larry and I visit, we'll perform the christening."

"Stop it! Just stop it!" Millie said, her hands flying to her ears again.

We wound through the wooded waterway, putting along and taking pleasure in the majestic red-tailed hawk we watched flying overhead. At the back of a small inlet on our right, a beaver smacked the water with his powerful tail, noisily warning us to steer clear of his home. Against the opposite bank, a row of assorted-sized turtles slid from their log perch as they saw us approaching.

Only once did we open up our throttles, and that was to shoot by Make-Out Cove. Moments later, I motioned right and we glided our Sea-Doos onto the beach and dismounted. We were completely sheltered in the blissful shadow of a high rock shelf that jutted out over that side of the beach. Another reason why this spot was one of my favorites.

Woods surrounded us. To the left, the landscape was almost as flat as the beach, with a very gradual climb to the craggy part of the shoreline.

The rock shelf that graced us with shade was the tip of a long expanse of dark gray stone that curved almost 90 degrees to form the towering walls of a deep, rounded pool so protected from the sun that the waters were chilly even in the middle of summer.

"Welcome to Bare Beach," I said, pulling off my t-shirt and wadding it into a ball.

"You wouldn't dare!" Millie yelped.

"I'm not disrobing, goofy," I said. "I'm making me a pillow so I can stretch out." I demonstrated by sitting down in the shallows, throwing my arms overhead, and positioning my clump of t-shirt beneath my head just out of the water.

"Ta-da!" I said, closing my eyes and sighing. "And FYI, dear cousin, Larry and I don't do any skinny-dipping when we're back here. We're kind of funny about keeping our clothes on in the great outdoors."

"Good to know," Millie responded. "'Cause somebody'd bound to show up and snap a pic of the Bargainomics Lady in her birthday suit!"

"Don't you know it!" I said.

Millie wandered over a few yards and chose her own spot, and we were soon sound asleep. It may have been moments or minutes, but we were both startled awake by the sound of an engine.

"What the heck?" Millie said.

"It's some sort of vehicle," I said. "Up there." I pointed toward the cliffs, even though we couldn't see a thing for the rock ledge hanging over us.

The sound grew louder and we could hear the snapping of limbs as the machine roared nearer. Brakes screeched and a puff of dust drifted out over the water. The engine was idling now. Who could be up there?

I signaled to Millie. She nodded understanding and we silently crept to our Sea-Doos. Pushing them off the sand, we walked them over as near the cliff wall as we dared, then pulled them onto the sand as far as we could. "We need to stay here," I whispered. "Whoever's up there can't see us."

Millie nodded again, too frightened to speak.

A door opened and a female voice said, "Well, Twon, my man, it's been real. I'll tell the kids their daddy *deeply* loved them." She gave a harsh laugh.

And then it clicked. Twon. Antoine. "It's the divers," I hissed, "and she's going to kill him!"

13

The door slammed and we heard the ground crunching beneath the rolling wheels. A loud metallic scrape caused us both to plug our ears. And then the splash. A splash so big it set a tsunami surging toward the rock wall and our tiny beach. We lunged for the Sea-Doos and held them in place until, as quickly as they'd come, the waves subsided.

Now there was only silence. We waited, stifling back sobs as we sat helpless, knowing a man was sinking to a watery grave only yards away from our hiding place.

And then we heard a splash. Not a very big one this time, but definitely a splash. And then the sound of swimming. Had she changed her mind and dove in to rescue him? Should we offer our assistance? We were paralyzed with fear.

"We can't go out there," I whispered, tears spilling down my cheeks. "That pool is practically bottomless. There's nothing we can do to help him."

"And she'll kill us too, if she sees us," Millie added, sobbing quietly.

We waited for what seemed an eternity, debating our next move. And then our decision was made for us. An aluminum fishing boat came charging out from the pool and shot past our hiding place without so much as a glance. One glimpse of that blue streak of hair and we knew it was the other diver driving that boat.

"They found the treasure!" Millie said. "And now she's going to get away with it and murder!"

"Not if we can help it," I said. "These Sea-Doos are a lot faster than that old fishing boat. Hang on a second."

I snatched my phone from my Sea-Doo's storage and pounded in 9-1-1. "What!" I groaned. "No signal." Dashing up the beach and onto the rocks, I yelped and ouched barefoot to the high point and tried again.

"9-1-1," said the operator. "What's your emergency?"

"A woman just pushed a vehicle into the lake, and there's a man inside," I screamed.

"What is your location, ma'am?" the calm voice of the operator asked.

"Smith Lake. Winston County. In the very back of the channel that leads to Make-Out Cove," I said.

"Would that be Bare Beach?" the man asked this time.

Sheesh. It did have a name. Millie had nailed it.

"Yes," I said. "And she's getting away."

"Ma'am," the operator said, "you need to remain calm and

stay where you are. I'm dispatching the Marine Police and the County Deputies now."

"But they'll never get here in time," I insisted. "And she's not getting away with murder."

"Please …"

I ended the call, tossed in my phone, slammed the seat, and ordered Millie, "Mount up. We've got a killer to catch."

We tore past Make-Out Cove, finally spotting Blue Streak as she steered her boat into the main channel. "Take that side!" I yelled to Millie, pointing right.

I gunned the engine even harder, blew well past Blue Streak, then performed a 180, pointing the Sea-Doo directly at the bow of her boat before cutting the throttle.

Flailing wildly and, likely, using words I was glad I couldn't hear, Blue Streak screamed for me to get out of her way. When she saw I wasn't complying, she swerved to her right—my left—and started around me. I hit the gas and shot across in front of her, barely missing the nose of her boat.

This time I could hear her. "Are you crazy, lady? Get outa my way!"

"No, you stop right where you are!" I yelled back.

"You …" Her sentence was much longer, but that's the only word I can put in print.

Our little exchange distracted her while Millie pulled up to her other side. Now we had her hemmed in. This chick was going nowhere.

Until she pulled her pistol. "Gun!" I screamed, slamming down on the accelerator as she aimed at me and fired. That's when Millie rammed Blue Streak's boat and sent chick and pistol flying. Blue Streak landed hard, but managed to stay in the boat. The gun, however, flew out over the water in a graceful arc before plummeting into the deep.

"Way to go, cuz!" I yelled, knowing there was no way she could hear me.

I did another 180 and roared back toward Millie and Blue Streak. Blue Streak had her outboard at full throttle, but her 40 horsepower was no match for the 155 horses Millie and I each had beneath us.

Blue Streak was still running, or puttering, I should say, as Millie now leisurely rode along beside her. Pulling up on the opposite side from Millie, I cruised along with them.

"It's useless, you know," I yelled. "Cops are on their way."

"Yeah, right," Blue Streak said, still floorboarding her getaway boat.

"And we saw you push Antoine in and drown him!" Millie yelled from the other side. Honest Abe corrected herself, "All right, we didn't exactly see it, but we heard it. And any way you slice it, you drowned him!"

"I didn't drown that moron!" Blue Streak screamed. "He was already dead!"

"Oh, yeah!" I yelled back. I bet Millie's throat was getting as sore as mine was. "And how do you suppose that happened? That gun you just tried to shoot me with?"

"So what?" Blue Streak laughed. "Where's the gun? At the bottom of the lake! Nobody'll ever find it!"

"Wrong!" screamed Millie. "It's right out from the Bartlett's boathouse!"

"Cuz!" I shouted. "You're awesome!"

"A clear head under pressure!" she called back.

By now, my throat had had it. And running so close together at this speed was an accident waiting to happen. The Marine Police needed to get here. And quickly.

Lo and behold, my unspoken prayer was answered. The flashing light atop the white boat zipping toward us told me the Marines were on the way. And not a moment too soon. My Sea-Doo began to cough and lurch, sputtering on its last drop of fuel just as Millie peeled away from Blue Streak, and Officer Jackson's voice crackled to life on his loudspeaker.

"Shut off your engine now!" he demanded. The rifle that Wetsuit—that is, Officer Osgood—was aiming at Blue Streak was also persuasive.

Blue Streak cut the throttle and Osgood leaned out and wrapped a rope around one of her boat's cleats. Stepping onto the fishing boat, he pulled her to her feet, yanked her hands behind her back, and slapped on a pair of handcuffs. With some assistance from Jackson, the scrawny blonde was loaded into their boat.

Millie pulled up next to my conked-out Sea-Doo and tossed me a rope. "We need to hear what's happening," she said.

With me in tow, Millie tied off to Jackson's boat, completing our floating collection of watercraft. "Ladies, we meet again," Jackson said. "And I believe you know this lady," he nodded to his prisoner. "And in her case, I use the term *lady* very loosely."

"She did try to shoot me," I said, "but we haven't been properly introduced."

"Then allow me the honor," Jackson said. "Meet Barbara Jean—also known as B.J.—Hyche. She and her other half, Antoine Dixon, have been a pain in my backside for quite a few years. But this time, I think she's outdone herself."

"B.J.!" Millie interjected. "That's the name we heard Friday night."

"That's it!" I said. Turning to Jackson, I continued. "You, literally, don't know the half of it. We saw ..."

"Heard ..." Millie corrected.

"She put Antoine in a vehicle and sunk him in the lake," I said before Millie could interrupt again.

"Is he ..." Jackson began.

It was my time to interrupt. "He was already dead," I said. "At least I hope so. We thought she pushed him in alive, but she just now told us he was already dead. She shot him. With the same gun she fired at me," I added indignantly.

"Where's the weapon now?" Jackson asked.

"In the lake," Millie answered. "But I believe a good diver can find it. I can show you the spot where it went in. Or maybe you'd like to handle that job personally, B.J.?"

Once again, I am unable to put Ms. Hyche's response in writing.

"All right, you two," Jackson said, "I'll need you to show me exactly where the vehicle went into the lake."

"Unless you plan on towing my Sea-Doo and B.J.'s boat," I said, "I'm going to need some gas for my Sea-Doo. And Millie's probably needs topping off too."

"Osgood," Jackson barked, "get Bargain Lady and her cousin some gas."

"Bargainomics Lady," I said. I'd let it slide at our first meeting. Not this time.

He ignored me and continued. "And when you're finished with that, run B.J.'s boat—which, by the way, ain't hers—over to Rock Ledge Marina. It was reported as stolen this morning," he added for my and Millie's benefit. "Radio for Ames to meet you there with a trailer. And contact the owners and tell them the boat'll need to be temporarily impounded as evidence. I'm taking Hyche with me and I'll turn her over to Winston County."

"Yes, sir," Osgood responded.

"And could we please have some water?" I asked. "We've yelled our throats dry."

"Before you take off in that boat," Millie said to Osgood, "you'll need to secure that bag in the bottom."

"Why?" asked Osgood. "What's in it?"

"Gold," Millie said. "Sixty pounds of it, we think."

"You're pulling my leg," Osgood snorted.

"No, we're not!" I said. I stood, straddling the Sea-Doo, and pulled B.J.'s boat close enough for me climb in. "It's right here," I said, pulling open the drawstring of a heavy neoprene bag.

That was when B.J. began cackling. Hooting. She'd have probably slapped her knees if her hands hadn't been cuffed behind her.

"Those two are crazy!" B.J. said. "Gold! They're nuts. I ain't had no gun. I ain't killed nobody. And I sure ain't had no gold."

"We'll just see about that, missy," Millie snapped. "Show 'em, Judy."

"It's a wetsuit," I said. "The gold's not here."

"What gold?" Jackson demanded.

"It's a very long story," Millie said. "How about we tell you after we show you where she sunk Antoine."

Osgood buzzed off toward Rock Ledge Marina and the rest of us headed back to Bare Beach. We were still a long way off when we saw the first of all the flashing lights on the clifftop. There were at least three different law enforcement agencies—county, state, and Fall Creek had come out to get in on the action. An ambulance stood at the ready, along with the coroner's van, a wrecker big enough to haul up a Mack truck, and, unfortunately, a bevy of reporters.

"Looks like the gang's all here," Jackson said when we cut our engines and pulled up beside him.

"They've already got a diver in the water," I said, pointing to a figure surfacing near the wall of the pool where Antoine's coffin had gone under.

"Y'all gave the dispatcher your location. When they got here, it wasn't hard to figure out exactly where to look," Jackson said. "See that oil slick?"

We sat on our Sea-Doos, watching. The diver gave a signal and a man standing at the end of the precipice gave a thumbs-up.

"Hey, that's Adam!" I said. "He's my niece's husband. Well, technically, she's Larry's niece. But I claim her too. And we both claim Adam."

Leaning much too close to the edge for my comfort, Adam lowered a massive hook and cable over the side, which then began its slow descent down to the water. High above, the big wrecker's diesel engine chugged steadily as the reel of cable sang out.

"I can't believe that cable will hold the weight of an entire truck," Millie said.

"Oh, it'll hold that and more," I assured her. "That's Lyle Wrecker Service's biggest truck. When Larry and I were at their shop, Adam showed it to us. The cable alone weighs two pounds per foot, and just that hook is over 30 pounds. Adam knows his stuff. He's done a lot of underwater recoveries."

At last, the diver, who had disappeared underwater, popped up again and gave a different signal, which prompted Adam to stop feeding out cable. He went under again, resurfaced a few minutes later, and jerked one thumb upward several times.

Adam acknowledged the message and waited for the diver to swim a safe distance away before reversing the reel of cable. The wrecker's engine revved with the strain as the submerged vehicle rose toward the surface.

"Omigosh!" I gulped. "It's Reverend Pratt's truck."

The backend of the black Chevy pickup rose until the cab had also cleared the surface. As the winch hauled the truck higher and higher, the sun reached the front windshield, revealing the gory Aquaman Antoine and the wide orange band on one of his lifeless fingers.

"It was Antoine," I said. "He stole Reverend Pratt's truck. Look at the ring," I said to Millie.

"And she," I said, pointing at B.J., "was his accomplice."

"I didn't steal no truck," B.J. snapped, adding a long string of personal commentary concerning my and Millie's character. "What you gonna accuse me of next?"

"Sit tight," Jackson instructed me and Millie. "I can't take any more of her. I'm handing her off to Winston County. Don't go anywhere." He grabbed the boat radio's microphone and requested one of the officers on the bluff to meet him at Bare Beach. Backing his boat away from our Sea-Doos, he circled around the curve and was gone from sight.

Adam began motioning for us to move back. Understandably, he didn't want anyone at the bottom of that cliff in the unlikely event of his cable coming loose or giving way.

We swung around and puttered to the far wall of the pool, both of us using our left hand and foot to keep the Sea-Doos from slamming against the rocks. The wrecker engine revved and the truck, dangling like a kitten in its mother's mouth, inched its way up the rock face. At the top, the truck scraped and groaned as it cleared the lip of the cliff. Millie and I cringed, recalling the very similar sound we'd heard when the truck went into the water.

Once the myriad of law enforcement agencies had finished questioning us, we made our way over to Melanie Posten, fighting off a passel of other reporters who swarmed in like vultures, crowding us from every side. Pulling the blankets the EMTs had given us around our heads, we did our best to keep our faces covered. It was the only time I'd ever wished I had my own burka.

"Back off!" a stern voice directly behind us ordered, causing us both to jump like jacks-in-the-box. Sergeant Nussbaum to the rescue. Who'da thought it? With one hand on each of our backs, he guided us through the gauntlet and over to a police van. "Climb in," he said. "Nobody will bother you now."

Turning to a young woman in uniform, the sergeant barked out another command. "Murphy, don't let anyone near this van unless these ladies okay it. Do I make myself clear?"

Murphy all but clicked her heels as she snapped out, "Yes, sir!" and took her position outside our vehicle.

"Deputy Murphy," I called, cracking the door of the windowless rear compartment where we were seated. There is one person we'd like to speak to."

Moments later, Deputy Murphy slid open the van door and Melanie Posten hopped in. "Ladies," she said, "first of all, thank the Lord both of you are all right." She hugged us through our blankets. "And now I want to hear every detail." Which is precisely what we told her.

"And," I concluded, "if B.J. spills the beans about where she's stashed that gold, there'll be an even bigger story for your follow-up."

"Okay, gotta run, but here's a little confidential info you deserve to know. The first dead guy you found, Bobby Joe Benson, died from, and I quote, 'an intentional and brutal blow to the back of the head.' That's coming straight from the coroner. My investigator nose tells me this is all connected. Do NOT repeat this to anyone," she warned before climbing out and sliding the door shut.

Melanie fairly sprinted away to her news crew and the group piled into their SUV and sped away. They were going to have one heck of a story to tell this evening. Now if we could manage to get back to our Sea-Doos.

"Deputy Murphy," I called. "We need just one more favor."

While our blanket-wrapped selves brought up the rear, Deputy Murphy cleared our path, calling, "These two will need to be put in quarantine until we can determine what they were exposed to."

I'd never seen reporters move away from potential interviewees any faster. In no time, we had slipped down to our Sea-Doos and were headed to Jane's.

As soon as we docked, I pulled out my cell phone and called Larry, launching into everything that had happened. Millie, on the other side of the boathouse, was on her phone filling in Bill.

"We're coming up there," Larry said. "Bill's with me. We're at Whiter Than Snow and were working on some of the washers."

"Sweetie," I said, "I appreciate your concern more than I can say, but we really are fine. And exhausted. And what you're doing is important."

"If you don't want us to come up there, then you two come home," Larry persisted.

"Honey, we're both ready to be home," I said. "But we're pooped, and we've got laundry to do and a little cleanup, all of which is going to have to wait until tomorrow. As soon as we get done, though, we're on the road to Caufield Corner."

14

Millie verified she'd had a similar conversation with Bill and he'd agreed there was no need to come to our rescue at this point. She and I would be home at the earliest possible moment.

As we walked across the lawn, we could see that Hat had been busy. The grass was perfectly manicured, and he'd even given a trim to some of the shrubbery. I made a mental note to compliment him on his workmanship.

"Yum," said Millie. "Smell that! Hat's put something delicious-smelling on the grill."

Seeing us approaching, Hat, replete in a red apron and a genuine chef's hat, waved a spatula and called out, "Perfect timing!"

"Where'd you find that getup?" I asked, thumping his chef's hat as I leaned in to inhale the luscious scent of burgers.

"Found it in the pantry. Y'all look bushed. Did you wear yourselves out on those Sea-Doos?" he asked.

"You could say that," I told him.

"It's been an interesting day," Millie said. "Give us a minute to clean up a bit and we'll help you get everything ready."

"No need," Hat said. "I've got all the bases covered."

"Alrighty, then," I said. "We'll be back in a jiffy."

One peek at the screened porch and we both stopped dead in our tracks. The table was beautifully laid with a tan linen tablecloth and a centerpiece of ferns and roses surrounded by perfectly placed dishes and silverware. In addition to footed iced beverage glasses, Hat had placed a champagne flute by each setting, a linen napkin expertly tucked inside.

"Hat," I said, "this is amazing. You, Hat, are amazing."

He took a small bow and then made a shooing motion. "Scat, ladies. Dinner will be served *en un momento*."

In keeping with the luxurious table setting, Millie and I opted for sundresses. We did the best we could to whip our hair into some semblance of style, and agreed sans makeup was how we'd have to be.

When we returned to the porch, our chef had lost his apron and hat and now stood in the doorway in a gleaming white t-shirt and blue jeans. "Welcome to Che' Hat," he said in a terrible French accent that had us both giggling. Stepping to the table, he seated Millie before circling to do the same for me.

"Tonight's menu," he continued in the accent, "is cheeseburgers, French fries, baked beans, and zee *pièce de résistance*, what we at Che' Hat like to call leftover brownies."

Millie and I applauded.

"One moment," Hat said, remaining in character. He disappeared into the kitchen and returned with a dish towel draped over his arm, one hand holding the neck of an icy green bottle while the bottom rested against his other palm.

"Welch's, 2021," he announced. "It's been a very good year for grapes."

Thinking of the day's events, Millie and I burst out laughing. We were alive. We were well. We were here with someone who was becoming very dear to us. All in all, it truly had been a very good year.

"May I?" Hat asked, before removing the napkins from our champagne flutes and placing them in our laps. He poured a generous amount of sparkling grape juice into each glass, then took the third seat at the table for himself.

"A toast," he said, returning to his natural voice. "To new friends."

"To new friends," we echoed.

"And to two way cool old—I mean, mature—ladies," Hat added, saluting each of us with his glass.

"And to you, Hat," Millie said, "whose unexpected appearance, aside from a few early moments of terror, has brought these two old ladies nothing but joy."

"I'll drink to that," I said.

We clinked our glasses, and Hat gulped his down in one swallow before dashing to the kitchen and returning with an appetizer of chips and dip.

"Enjoy," he said, collecting our plates and heading for the kitchen. "Back with the main course in a minute."

Millie and I munched in silence, staring out at a brilliant sky of pinks and oranges as the sun disappeared behind the horizon.

Our maître d' had left the bottle with us, so I poured us all another round before breaking the silence. "A dead body."

"A dead murdered body," Millie interjected.

"Yes, and a carjacking," I said, "plus another dead body, which was also a murder victim. And being shot at by our second victim's killer. Am I leaving anything out?"

"A lot," Millie said. "But those suffice as the low points."

"What I mean," I said, "is that, even with all the bad stuff that's happened, it's been a wonderful getaway otherwise. Sure, if we hadn't come, we wouldn't have been involved in any of that, but we wouldn't have met Hat or Trish or Victor, either."

"Or Cooter," Millie reminded me.

"Or Cooter," I agreed. "In spite of the 'low points'," I air-quoted, "I'm so glad we came."

"I am too," Millie said. "This calls for another toast."

At that moment, Hat came out the door with a laden tray, which he placed on the smaller table by the doorway. He then delivered our plates, serving himself last, and took his own seat.

"One more toast," Millie insisted.

"All right by me," Hat said, lifting his glass and smiling.

"To all who, despite this week's trials and troubles, have been kept safe and brought together with new people to love," she said.

"Amen," I said, "and thank you, Jesus." First time I'd ever heard a toast turned into a blessing.

When we'd scraped the last morsels of food from our plates, Hat cleared our dishes and returned with coffee and brownies.

"I could really get used to this," I said. "Thank you, Hat." I reached over and squeezed his hand.

"Hey, it was fun for me too," he said, blushing. "We don't do up meals like this now that we live in the Village. It was nice to do it again. I may have been young, but I still remember."

"Did you have a cook?" Millie asked.

"Oh, yeah," he said. "Juanita. And a housekeeper, Margaret. And a groundskeeper, Mr. Bartholomew. He never let me call him by his first name."

"Your folks must miss having all those servants," I said.

"No doubt," said Hat. "But what they miss most are those friendships. Juanita, Margaret, and even Mr. Bartholomew were like family. It broke Mom's and Dad's hearts when they had to let them all go. Juanita and Margaret were live-ins. They didn't just lose their jobs. They lost their home. I still miss them."

"Did any of them stay in touch?" Millie asked.

"They all did, and still do," Hat said. "Dad wasn't in any shape to do much, and Mom could barely leave his side, but she made phone call after phone call, trying to find new situations for all of them. And finally, it paid off. Everybody ended up with new jobs working for good people. Juanita and Margaret were both hired by the same family."

"Your parents must be really special people," I said.

"They are," Hat said. "And when I finish college and get my engineering degree, I intend to buy them a house of their own and do whatever I can to help them."

"We know you will," Millie said. "Your parents raised a good son."

"So, enough about me," Hat said, his cheeks tinged pink by our praise. "Let's hear about your day."

"Whoa," said Hat as he rinsed another plate and I stuck it in the dishwasher. "That was not what I expected to hear."

"Yeah, well, it's not what we expected to be doing," Millie said as she put away the leftovers.

"You two are, like, heroes," Hat said, turning from the sink and giving a double thumbs-up.

"Two very tired ones," I said. "And before we forget to tell you, all three of us are evicted from here as of tomorrow. We've promised our husbands we're coming home, and you, young man, are going home too."

"I don't know," Hat said.

"I do," I said. "You've told us what wonderful parents you have. Don't keep them in the dark about what's happened with your truck. They might help you come up with a solution."

"Yeah, I guess you're right," Hat said. "I just don't want to give them something else to worry about."

"Parents are pretty good at handling stuff," Millie said. "And yours have already handled far more than most contend with in a lifetime. Give them some credit."

"And we'll take you home when we leave here tomorrow," I said.

"That's way out of your way," Hat said. "You don't need to do that."

"We may not need to, but we want to," Millie said. "You should never have gotten yourself tied up with us, Hat." She punched him lightly on the arm. "'Cause you're stuck with us now."

"You gonna watch the news?" Hat asked, dropping into the recliner and picking up the remote.

"I'll pass," I said. "We've already lived it. I don't need to see it again."

"I second that motion," Millie said.

"Stay up as late as you please," I told Hat. "The TV won't bother me as long as you don't have it blasting. And besides, I want to read a while before I call it a night."

"Me too," said Millie.

"Gee, Mom, does this mean I can even stay up past midnight?" Hat asked, a wicked grin on his face.

I grabbed a pillow from the sofa and sailed it across the room, making a direct hit on my target.

"Hey!" Hat yelled. "What was that for?" As if he didn't know.

"Good night," I said. "See you in the morning."

"G'night, Hat," Millie said. "And again, dinner was absolutely wonderful."

Tuesday morning *William Tell* woke me. My phone was ringing. I looked at the time—7:22—and glared at the caller. Or at least the caller's name. It was Jane.

"Hello," I said, struggling to sound somewhat coherent.

"Oh, did I wake you?" asked Jane. "I'm so sorry. I've been up since 5:30, so I guess I think everybody else has been too." Jane and all jolly morning people are hard to love—at least, they are before breakfast.

"That's okay," I said. "How are you and where are you?"

"We're in Atlanta. Got in yesterday evening. Cliff and I decided to come back a day early so we can do a little shopping. And," she added, "the concierge here managed to get us great seats to a show at the Fox Theatre this evening."

"Sounds like fun," I said.

"I mainly called to check in," Jane said. "Have you enjoyed your time at the lake? I hope there wasn't too much work for you to do."

"It's been eventful," I said, "but everything's fine." Talk about the understatement of the century.

"Oh?" Jane said, her voice taking on a hint of concern.

Ignoring the question in her voice, I prattled on. "We took the pontoon out. Went over to the marina and bottle-fed the carp. Fished off the pier. Rode the Sea-Doos. Swam. I'll tell you every detail once you're home."

Relief sounded in her voice. "Wonderful," she said. "When you said 'eventful,' I was afraid there'd been a problem. You know, I received texts from both my girls about some horrible murder on the lake. I almost didn't mention it. Didn't want to put a damper on your getaway. But I suspect you've already seen it on the news."

"We did," I said. "Such a terrible thing."

"Yes, it was," Jane agreed. "The lake is usually such a safe and restful place." Changing the subject, she asked, "Has my yard man been there? He's the nicest young fellow. Hadley Vincent. I wrote his name on the magnetic notepad on the refrigerator."

Our bad for not reading the fridge notes. "He has," I said. "And he does seem like a very nice person." Who had a lot of explaining to do when he made his confession to Jane.

"Well, I won't keep you," Jane said. "I've already taken up too much of your time."

"Not at all," I said. "We'll be leaving here shortly …" I began.

Jane interrupted. "I thought you and Millie were staying until Thursday. I promise you Cliff and I won't be there before

Thursday afternoon."

"Oh, no," I assured her, "I think both our husbands are ready to have us come home." Insistent was more like it. "I'll put the key back in the barbecue tool case. Call me when you get home and have had a minute to rest."

Jane chuckled. "A minute's about all we'll have. We'll fly home first thing in the morning, catch our breath, and then drive up to the lake, stopping, of course, to pick up enough groceries to feed our growing army." Between Jane and Cliff's four children, there were nine grandkids, plus the eldest granddaughter and her husband were expecting their second child.

"I don't know how you do it," I said, meaning it.

"At my age, you mean?" Jane said. "The same as I did when I was your age, Judy. Only slower." We both got a good laugh out of that one. "Okay, my dear, I'll call you sometime tomorrow," Jane promised.

I looked over at Millie's side of the bed, surprised she hadn't already thrown a pillow at me for not leaving the room to take the phone call. Millie was nowhere to be seen, so I tapped on the bathroom door before entering and finding it unoccupied. After I'd washed my face and taken care of the other necessities, I dressed, came back into the bedroom, and stripped the linens from our bed. The faster I got these into the washer, the faster we could finish up and go home.

Millie and Hat were already making breakfast. "Good morning," the cheery duo called.

"Good morning," I responded. "Y'all sure are early birds this morning."

"Yeah, well, I think I zonked out right after you gave me permission to stay up," Hat grinned.

"And you were still buried in your book when I called it a night," Millie said.

"I didn't stay up much longer than you did," I told Millie. "What are y'all fixing, and what can I do to help?"

"French toast and link sausages," Hat announced. "Pour some juice, round up silverware and napkins, and we should be good to go. Carafe of coffee is already on the porch."

"Let me throw these sheets in the washer and I'll get right on it," I said.

In the laundry, the washer and dryer were already at work. The baskets Millie and I had filled to overflowing with the linens we'd stripped from the beds last Thursday were both empty. There wasn't a speck of dirty laundry to be seen.

"Has the laundry fairy been here or what?" I asked when I returned to the kitchen.

"What do you mean?" Millie asked.

"What happened to all the bedding we needed to wash?" I asked. "It's not in there."

"Don't ask me," said Millie.

"I washed all that while y'all were out saving the world yesterday," Hat said. "It's in the linen closet. Threw my bed stuff in when I got up this morning—it's in the dryer now. And I dumped that basketful of towels into the washer a few minutes ago."

"That was so thoughtful of you, Hat," I said. "Do you realize what this means?" I asked.

"We won't be stuck here doing laundry for half the morning?" Millie countered.

"Exactly," I said. "And since Hat is the reason we won't be sitting here for hours waiting to change washer and dryer loads, we should reward him and ourselves with a final pontoon ride out on the lake."

"I like your thinking," said Hat. "I haven't been on a boat in a long time. Unless you count sleeping on one," he added, smiling.

As soon as we finishing eating, I headed back to the laundry room and removed Hat's sheets from the dryer. Shifting the towels from the washer to the dryer, I put the final load of sheets into the washer.

In the kitchen, I presented Hat with his bed's clean linens. "Get these on your bed, then come upstairs and help me and Millie make these other beds," I instructed.

"Teamwork," I said, as Millie and I put the finishing touches on the first upstairs bedroom. The queen bed and daybed with trundle were now ready for Jane's family.

Hat appeared in the doorway. "Show me what sheets go where and I'll get started on the next room," he said.

"Hat and I can tackle the double bunk beds," Millie said. "They're the hardest to make up, and he's younger and more agile than we are."

"And I'll get the other two rooms," I said. "They're both queen beds and easier to fool with. We can do the final run-through on everything else when we get back."

15

Hat, who made it very clear he'd have preferred to take the Sea-Doos, was pacified by being designated our captain. "Aye, aye," he said, turning his ever-present ball cap around and taking over the console. "Where to?" he said.

"You're the captain," I responded. "But I would like to make a stop up here where we saw B.J. and Antoine." Under my direction, Hat motored us right to the spot, nosing the pontoon toward the shoreline.

"Hold up," I said. "Just ease us in enough for me and Millie to step off on that ledge," I said, referring to a shelf about a foot underwater at the shoreline. "Then keep the boat out here until we come back. We've already scraped a place on one of the Sea-Doos during that ordeal with B.J. We don't want to have to tell Jane we damaged her pontoon too."

"But I'd like to come with y'all," Hat argued.

"There's probably nothing to see, besides a deserted campsite," I said. "Give us a few minutes. If we find anything interesting, we'll yell."

"And then what?" Hat persisted.

"You can find a good sandy spot to park the boat," Millie said, showing her lack of nautical terms. "But if you do, make sure you tie it off so it doesn't float away."

"Okay," Hat conceded, begrudgingly.

Millie and I picked our way back to the deer trail and were soon at the campsite.

"What are we looking for?" Millie asked.

"I don't really know," I said. "It's just my radar."

Millie and, even more so, Larry, were familiar with my "radar." My instincts had been wrong a few times, but far more often than not, I was right. Whether, as in the case of our meeting Cooter, it was a stop at an unpromising-looking flea market, or my discovery of out-of-the-way eateries or shops, my radar rarely failed me.

We began searching the camp from top to bottom, promising to actually report the location to Sergeant Nussbaum once we had finished.

"And there's no need to mention this being our second time to be here," Millie said.

"Definitely not something to bring up," I said.

We emptied the ice chest, shook out the sleeping bags, and

finally resorted to taking down their tent so we could check out the ground underneath it. "It'd be a pretty smart place to bury that gold," I said, as we pulled the tent to one side and folded back the protective ground cover. Nothing indicated the soil beneath had been loosened.

Next, we targeted the fire ring. "Who, besides us, would look here?" Millie said. "If I were hiding gold, this would be my choice spot."

But after dragging the fire ring and its load of ashes aside, we didn't find anything.

Shoving the ice chest over to the hanging food supplies, I pulled down on the limb until I could just reach the top of the bag. Millie positioned herself to help and, using the diver's knife we'd found in the tent, I cut the rope and we lowered the heavy mesh bag to the ground. Inside were canned goods and a host of other food staples. But not a speck of gold.

I spun in a slow circle, surveying everything around us. "That gold could be anywhere around here," I said, waving my hand at the densely forested landscape. "Or it could be nowhere near here. One more sweep and I give up."

"And Hat's probably getting impatient," said Millie.

"Let's widen our circle," I said. "Let's go out another 20 yards or so from the clearing and see what we find."

"Lions, tigers, and bears, most likely," Millie said, "and a few rattlesnakes, copperheads, and let's not forget the occasional cottonmouth. And I don't think these water shoes are snakeproof," she concluded, lifting a foot for my inspection.

"Girl, we grew up playing in the Alabama woods. How many times were either of us snakebit?" I asked.

"We were younger and faster then," Millie countered.

"Oh, good grief," I snorted. "You take that side and I'll take this one." And for pure meanness, I added, "We're more likely to get covered up with ticks than see a snake out here."

"You're a terrible person," Millie said, "in case I've never told you."

She picked up a hefty stick and started her trek into the wilderness. I did likewise.

I'd covered about half my section when Millie called out, "I found something! Bring the knife and the ice chest."

Crashing through the underbrush, I hit the clearing, snatched up the ice chest and knife, and shoved my way through the bushes. "What is it?" I asked, when I finally reached Millie.

"Look up," she said. Suspended from a limb was another mesh bag. Flies and some very scary wasps and yellow jackets swarmed around it. Crawling all over it were at least a gazillion fire ants.

"Garbage," I said. "That's why they hung it this far from their camp, and that's why all these critters are after it."

"Yep," said Millie. "And what better way to keep people away from a bag of gold than to hide it inside a giant bag of garbage?"

"Point taken," I said. "But we're going to need reinforcements. "Wait here."

"No, thank you," Millie said. "You wait here with the deadly swarm. I'll be back in a minute."

I pulled the ice chest some distance from the dangling bag, sat down, and waited. The outer bag was a heavy duty mesh with a regular plastic trash bag inside it. I hoped whatever we discovered wasn't throw-up gross. Whatever it was, we were about to find out.

Hat came crashing through the bushes, armed with a giant can of flying insect spray he'd found on the pontoon. Larry and I, having personally fished too close to a wasp nest, had learned it was a handy item to keep on board.

"Stand back, ladies," Hat said. "I've got this."

Millie and I moved almost back to the clearing as we watched Hat do battle with the teeming horde. "We'd better wait a few minutes and make sure I took 'em all out," Hat said as he sprinted back to the campsite. "If there are any survivors, they'll be looking for payback."

We waited, then allowed our knight in shining t-shirt to take the lead as we re-approached the garbage. "Gimme the knife," Hat said, taking the weapon from my hand.

He stretched to his limit, but even with the ice chest to stand on, the rope was too high up to reach. "Looks like we'll have to do this the hard way," Hat said, beginning a sawing motion across the bottom of the bag.

The first stab into the trash bag brought an overwhelming stench and an ooze of putrefied garbage. "Stop," I said. "I can't stand it."

"Aw, come on," Hat said. "I'm getting the worst of the smell.

And I'll help clean it up, I promise. Just one more stab, just to be sure I didn't miss anything."

"One more," I said, "and then we clean up what's fallen and get out of here."

Carefully standing to one side so as not to wear the falling refuse, Hat peered upward into the bag. "Looks like there's another bag inside this one," he said. With that, he plunged the knife upward and deep.

The whole bag seemed to shudder, like the throes of a foul-breathed dragon. The interior bag gave way, and a brilliant gold shower began to rain down.

"We found it!" we shouted in unison.

Forgetting the lions, tigers, bears, snakes, and ticks, Millie barreled through to the campsite, scooped up the neoprene bag we'd taken the knife from, and rushed back. "Here," she said. "We can put the gold in this."

Thus began our retrieval of Dixon's Treasure. Fortunately, when Hat stabbed the interior bag containing the gold, it had begun sliding toward the bottom of the outer bag as the gold spilled out, eventually forming a precarious plug that kept the rest of the garbage from falling.

"We'll take the outer areas," Millie told Hat. "You gather what's directly under the bag."

"You mean, the gold that's covered in crap," he said.

"You got it," Millie said. "Anything with 'crap' on it goes in the ice chest. We'll rinse it before we put it in with the rest."

Hat, realizing there was no easy way to handle his part of our salvage job, dug in with both hands and began tossing gold into the ice chest. We were still finding pieces several feet away after he'd cleared his section to smooth dirt. With a perfunctory swipe of his hands using leaves and dirt, Hat joined in searching the perimeter.

"Whoa!" he suddenly called, bringing us both to a standstill.

"What is it?" I asked, half expecting him to yell, "Snake!"

"Y'all need to see this," he said.

Millie and I hurried to his location. "What? What?" we said.

"That," Hat answered, pointing to a large, dark brown stain in the soft, sandy earth. A foot or so from the stain, a cantaloupe-sized rock was thickly coated with the same dark substance.

"Blood," Millie said, shivering as she said it.

"And I think that's hair," Hat said, using a stick to indicate a matted clump on the bloodstained rock. "That must be how B.J. killed Antoine."

"Nope," I said. "Not buying it. I mean, if you had a gun, what would you do?" I held out both hands, weighing the choices. "Rock, pistol, rock, pistol?"

"Yeah, and she pretty much admitted to us that she shot him," Millie added. "Besides, Antoine was a big guy. I don't think she'd have risked smacking him with a rock and only making him mad. Count on it. His corpse is sporting one or two bullet holes."

"Makes sense," Hat said. "But somebody got their head bashed in with this rock. And nobody could have survived that much blood loss."

"That's it!" I said, my radar kicking in again. "I'm betting that 'somebody' was Bobby Joe Benson."

For a split second, Millie looked puzzled, and then she had her light bulb moment. "B.J.!" she said. "Not just Barbara Jean, but Bobby Joe! He could have been one of the people we heard out on the water Friday night."

"Exactly," I said. "There's only one problem with that theory."

"What?" Millie asked.

"He was already dead by then. And we already know he didn't accidentally fall off that cliff. Somebody murdered him, and I believe it took place right here," I said.

"Somehow or other, he was mixed up in this too, and one or both of them decided to cut him out of the deal. Then, whichever one of them killed him, or maybe the two of them together, took his body around to Make-Out Cove and dumped it off the cliff. I bet that's exactly what happened."

"Had to have been Antoine," Hat said. "Barbara Jean would've used her pistol."

"A pistol I'm guessing Antoine didn't know she had. A pistol she had already planned to use on 'Twon'," I said, making air quotes with my fingers, "as soon as they found the gold. Thank the Lord they didn't decide to do away with Cooter."

"For sure," Millie agreed. "Barbara Jean not only committed murder, but premeditated murder. And Antoine was a murderer

210

too. We've got to call the police and let them know about this crime scene."

"At this point, there's no rush," I said. "If we're right and Antoine's who killed him, the only other question will be if Barbara Jean played any part in it. Right now, let's clean up this gold, deliver it to Sergeant Nussbaum, and give him our info. We've got to go to Fall Creek to take Hat home anyway."

"The police aren't going to be happy with the way we went through this campsite," Millie said.

"But at least we didn't contaminate the rock or blood stain evidence. The rest, they'll just have to live with," I said.

"Right," said Hat. "It's not like y'all knew this was a murder scene when you started ripping it apart."

"Right," I said. "And with your way with words, I think your task at the station is to remain silent and let us do the talking. You," I said, "stick to your name, rank, and serial number."

Hat hoisted the ice chest-cum-treasure chest. Millie and I both kept a firm grip on the bag with the rest of the gold. We lugged our loads back to the campsite and paused to catch our breath.

"Gimme just a second," Hat said. "You're not the only one with radar," Hat added, winking at me.

Following the faint tire tracks leading away from the camp, Hat jogged out of sight. He wasn't gone long before we caught sight of him again, this time moving in our direction. He bent forward, hands on knees, panting.

"I know why they stole the truck," he said. "Theirs," he

pointed in the direction he'd just come from, "busted an axle. It hit, like, a boulder, and, snap! Dead on the spot. Those guys were in need of another set of wheels."

Hat led us to where he had beached the pontoon, then with Millie as lookout, he and I took on the disgusting task of washing the gold in the ice chest. That done, we added the cleaned gold to the bag with the rest of it, loaded it onto the pontoon, and sped back to Jane's.

"First things first," I said as Hat hoisted the bag of gold and started across the lawn. "Wait by the car, Hat. I'll be right out."

I hurried inside, grabbed my keys, and dashed outside. Unlocking the Hyundai, I raised the hatch and Hat heaved in our treasure.

"All right," I said, "let's make record time. Straighten up everything that needs straightening. Check the washer and dryer. Millie, put the sheets on our bed. Hat, empty the washer and run the vacuum. I'll clean out the fridge and take the trash out."

"And for goodness' sake," Millie said, "let's all hit the shower before we leave. Jane won't mind a few dirty towels being left behind, but Sergeant Nussbaum would definitely mind having our smelly selves inside his station."

We finished our clean-a-thon, both house-wise and personal, and piled into the car for the ride to Fall Creek. We breezed through the metal detector and up to the desk where Nussbaum glanced up, did a double take, and frowned.

"Ladies," he said. "You're back. And with reinforcements."

"Yes, we are," I said. "Sergeant Nussbaum, we need you or some other officer to accompany us to our car. We have something you need to see, and we weren't sure it was safe to bring it through the metal detector."

"And you say I have a way with words?" Hat whispered.

Within seconds, we were surrounded by at least four officers. "Now," said Nussbaum, "would you be so kind as to show these officers what you're talking about?"

"Sure," I said, and Millie and Hat turned to followed me out of the station.

"Uh-uh-uh," the sergeant said. "You two take a seat. And you," he said to Millie, "start talking."

By the time Nussbaum heard our entire story and the other officers had shown him that we, indeed, possessed a 60-pound bag of gold, his tone had gone from one of patronization to undisguised amazement.

"I've heard of Dixon's Treasure my whole life," Nussbaum said. "Fantasized about it as a kid. Never believed a word of it as an adult. And now, here I sit, staring right at it." We were all seated around a table in one of the interrogation rooms.

One of the other officers who'd sat in on our interviews suddenly pushed his laptop across to Nussbaum and said, "Take a look at this."

213

The sergeant studied the screen for a couple minutes, murmuring, "Well, I'll be darn. Well, I'll be darn," every few seconds. Finally, he spun the screen around for us to see.

"Your crazy story checks out," he said. "Dixon must have been the one who stole that statue out of that temple. And here's some news: there are two rewards offered for the return of the statue. Some guy named Yi Kang-Dae is offering $50,000 for the statue's return."

"We didn't exactly find the statue in one piece," I said.

"No, but the South Koreans aren't going to turn up their noses at the return of 60 pounds of pure gold, either. Says here there's a five percent finder's fee, based on the gold's current value," said Nussbaum.

"Who knows what 60 pounds of gold is worth these days?" said Millie.

"I can answer that," said Hat, whose thumbs had been whizzing around his phone screen. "First of all, gold is weighed in Troy pounds, not regular pounds. Sixty pounds translates to about 73 Troy pounds, so we're talking in the ball park of $1,643,169."

"I can't believe it!" Millie and I yelped.

"That's, that's, that's ..." Millie stammered.

"A lot of money," I said.

"Which makes the five percent finder's fee $82,158.45," said Hat, grinning broadly. "Split two ways, you ladies are going to have a nice chunk of change."

"Two ways, my eyeball!" I exclaimed. "Hat, one-third of that money is yours."

"And we won't take 'no' for an answer," Millie added.

"I-I don't know what to say," Hat gulped, his eyes starting to water.

"Then don't say anything," I told him. "You deserve it."

16

We dropped Hat in front of an apartment in the worst-looking government housing project I'd ever seen.

"Don't y'all want to come in and meet my parents?" Hat pleaded.

"You're on your own for this one, buddy," I said. "I promise we'll come back and make our introductions soon, but today you need to face the music by yourself."

"Your folks have already handled so much, I don't think finding out their son has been involved in some minor criminal activities is going to send them over the edge," added Millie.

"And none of your other news, either," I said. "Besides, you can catch them off guard by first regaling them with your treasure-hunting adventure."

We made sure Hat actually went inside the apartment before we drove away from the squalid neighborhood. Already, Millie and I had made a decision.

My daddy was the ninth of ten children. Consequently, I have a slew of cousins—31, only counting first cousins—which means I have a family member in pretty much any occupation you care to name, from sewer worker to NASA engineer, literally. It was to Cousin Dennis that Millie and I turned with plans for our reward money. When we explained what we wanted to do, he was eager to help and promised he'd handle our request personally and discreetly.

When I finally rolled into my own driveway, I was happily exhausted. It'd been a long day, but wrapping up at the lake and taking care of business with Dennis was worth every minute it had taken. Opening my car door, I smelled the tantalizing fragrance of steaks on the grill and saw my adorable hubby plating the first juicy T-bone.

"Now that's timing," he called. "Let me put this in the warming oven and I'll help you bring in your things." My steak always comes up first since I prefer medium rare and Larry likes his steak pretty much charcoal. That may be a slight exaggeration, but believe me, when Larry cooked a steak to his liking, there was assuredly no life left in it.

After piling everything in a heap in the den floor, I brought out the salad and bread while Larry added steaming hot baked potatoes to our plates. Napkins, silverware, glasses, and a pitcher of iced tea were already on the table, along with a selection of condiments including sour cream, shredded cheese, and Larry's strange-but-true favorite baked potato topping: raw honey.

"Oh, sweetie, this looks wonderful," I told him. "And smells marvelous. Thank you so much for doing this."

"Thank you so much for coming home in one piece," Larry returned. "After all these years, I've kinda gotten used to having you around."

"Is that so?" I said teasingly as he pulled out my chair, seated me, and bent to kiss my neck in a way that still made me shiver. I reached for his hand and brought it to my lips and kissed it. "I do love you," I said.

"And I love you," he echoed. "Now let's enjoy this celebratory meal. Afterwards, there's dessert and coffee and we'll see what else that might lead to." He wiggled his eyebrows suggestively.

"Lead away," I grinned, winking and reaching for his hand again.

As always, we bowed our heads together. "You lead," I whispered. And Larry prayed a sweet and simple prayer thanking the Lord for our blessings and for His protection over me and Millie during all our ordeal.

"Amen," we said in unison.

After dinner, I showered and reappeared in one of my favorite sleep shirts. "Your dessert is served, madam," Larry announced, patting the seat beside him on the sofa. Spread across the coffee table were a carafe of coffee, our cups, and two plates of what I recognized as our neighbor Clarice's Ooey-Gooey Chocolate Cake.

"Sweetheart, you can make this dessert for me anytime," I said, plopping down beside him and accepting the plate he proffered. "And I'll have to thank Clarice too," I added. "I suspect she might have had something to do with this."

"Mmft," Larry said through a mouthful of cake. I think that translated as "might."

Drawing my feet up and snuggling closer to Larry, I sighed contently. "It feels so good to be home."

"And I like knowing you're here where I can keep an eye on you," Larry said, leaning in to face me.

"Trust me," I said, kissing him lightly on the lips, "I don't plan on being anywhere near a crime scene again. Ever," I firmly added.

"I'd like to think you didn't plan on it this time," Larry said.

"You know what I mean," I said, making a face at my husband.

The barrage of commercials ended and Larry unmuted the sound in time to hear Melanie Posten's intro into her special report. The viewers who were waiting to see WEEE's popular sitcom, "Hopeless," were going to be upset that their show was being preempted, but I was sure this was one news special that would keep them glued to the channel.

"I'm here on the steps of the Winston County Sheriff Department's building with the latest information on a developing

219

story. Earlier this afternoon, accused murderer Barbara Jean Hyche was brought into this building in handcuffs, escorted by two Winston County deputies." The video showed a bedraggled B.J. Hyche walking between the two officers, her head down and her feet still bare.

I snatched up my phone and fired off a text to Millie: "It's on. R U watching? Turn on WEEE."

"This unfolding drama began on Thursday morning, when the Reverend Victor Pratt," Melanie continued, as a steady stream of police and reporters milled in and out through the glass doors behind her, "arrived at Simmons Chapel Community Church to begin a typical day in his office. What was first believed to have been two masked men forced him to hand over his truck and then sped away in it.

"Since that time, WEEE has learned that a body discovered in Lewis Smith Lake later that same day is believed to be connected with everything we're about to disclose to you. That body," Melanie said, as the blurry video of the body on the ledge in Make-Out Cove appeared on the screen, "has now been identified as Bobby Joe Benson." A mug shot of the victim appeared on the screen.

"According to the Winston County coroner, Dr. Lizzie Okada, Benson died after being intentionally and brutally struck on the head. This morning, Reverend Pratt's 1997 Chevy pickup was discovered in Lewis Smith Lake. Inside was the dead body of Antoine Dixon, believed to be one of the two individuals who carjacked the reverend. Hyche, whom you just saw being escorted into the sheriff's station, is now suspected of not only being Dixon's accomplice in the carjacking, but also his killer." A mug shot of Dixon from a prior arrest appeared on the screen.

"While autopsy results are still pending, Dixon is believed to have been killed before the pickup, with his body inside it, was rolled into the lake. According to sources who knew both Dixon and Hyche, the two had been in a long and volatile relationship. That relationship is believed to have ended in Hyche murdering Dixon, the father of her two children, and then attempting to make an escape with a fortune in gold she and Dixon had recovered from an underwater cave in Lewis Smith Lake.

"Early in July, the couples' three-year-old daughter and five-year-old son were removed from the family's home by social services after an altercation brought police to the residence and a substantial amount of illegal drugs and weapons were discovered. Dixon and Hyche were both out on bond, awaiting trial on these charges.

"So how did 60 pounds of gold end up beneath the waters of Lewis Smith Lake?" Melanie asked. "To answer that question, we have to go back decades, to 1953 when 26-year-old Army Corporal Henry Dixon returned home at the end of his stint in South Korea." A snapshot of a handsome young soldier appeared beside Melanie's right shoulder, and the banner beneath it identified the man as Henry Dixon.

"But only weeks after arriving in Alabama, Corporal Dixon

was on his way home from an illegal gambling and drinking establishment on the outskirts of Fall Creek when, according to a report WEEE pulled from case records maintained by the Fall Creek Police Department, he staggered out in front of a passing car and was critically injured.

"His young wife was brought to the scene and, as he was being loaded into an ambulance, he was overheard telling her, 'You and the boy will be fine. Everything you need is in Swallow Canyon.' And then he passed out. Sadly, Corporal Dixon died on the way to the hospital without ever regaining consciousness.

"Swallow Canyon was a small valley surrounded on three sides by steep rock walls," Melanie explained while a pair of topographical maps shared opposite halves of the screen behind her. "Mickey Anderson is in the studio to explain these graphics. Mickey, tell us the significance of these two maps, please."

"Sure will, Melanie," Mickey's voice said as Melanie disappeared and only the maps remained onscreen. "The topographical map on your left," the disembodied voice continued, "is from 1953. As you can see," Mickey continued, a circle suddenly appearing near the lower left of the map, "Swallow Canyon was located right here."

Switching to the right-hand map, he continued. "But in 1961, this entire area …"—a much bigger circle appeared on the right-hand map—"… including Swallow Canyon, became part of 21,000-acre Lewis Smith Lake, a manmade Alabama Power reservoir. That was eight years later, though, Melanie. How come the gold wasn't found before the land was flooded?"

"Good question, Mickey," Melanie responded, reappearing onscreen at the Sheriff's building. "Corporal Dixon's cryptic message meant nothing to his wife. She searched land records to see if he had secretly bought property there, especially since there were already rumors of the area being bought as part of what would be flooded to create the lake.

"But Mrs. Dixon never found anything. James, the Dixons' son, grew up hearing about his father's dying words. As a young boy, he became fascinated with the TV show *Sea Hunt*, eventually joining the Navy and becoming what was then termed a frogman, an underwater diver. He made a 20-year career of the Navy, returning home at every opportunity to spend his time diving around the flooded region that had been Swallow Canyon.

"He, like his mother, filled his own son's ears with stories about the hidden treasure, and it was James who concluded that the treasure had to be something cached in one of the many caves along the canyon walls. Through the years, he tried to explore every inch of Swallow Canyon, but his efforts were all unsuccessful. Like his father before him, he left behind a son, Zachary, who, despite his mother never mentioning the treasure, spent his very brief lifetime obsessed with finding it. Again, without success.

"However, one generation later, Henry's great-grandson, Antoine Dixon, along with Barbara Jean Hyche, finally found the narrow niche where gold, valued at over one and a half million dollars, was hidden away on dry land years before Lewis Smith Lake came into existence."

Larry hit the pause button. "A million and a half dollars!" Larry whistled. "Even a five percent finder's fee is nothing to sneeze at."

"For sure," I agreed. "Let's listen." I snagged the remote and pressed "play."

"Since WEEE began looking into the story of Dixon's Treasure, we've learned that the Dixon Gold, as it's now being called, is said to be cursed. Henry Dixon died at only 26 years of age. His son James, an experienced Navy diver, died in 1990 at the age of 40 after suffering a massive heart attack following a dive near Pago Pago in American Samoa." A photo of James Dixon in full diving gear popped onscreen.

"The only son in Henry Dixon's third generation, Zachary Dixon, died in a mining accident in 1995 when he was only 20, just one month before the birth of his only child, Antoine." A photo of Zachary Dixon briefly appeared beside Melanie.

"The last known piece of what we know about this puzzle concerns how Henry Dixon acquired this valuable cache of gold and how we believe he smuggled it home from South Korea," Melanie continued. "But before I reveal that final piece of information, let me bring us back to what's happened in the last few days and even hours.

"Once the gold had been retrieved, Antoine Dixon's life was apparently of no value to Ms. Hyche. She is believed to have driven the stolen pickup to the Bare Beach area with Dixon inside, either killing him there, or having already killed him before driving the truck to the clifftop. Leaving Dixon's dead body inside, she then put the truck in gear and watched it plunge into the water.

"Having already stolen a small fishing boat, it is thought that she dove from the cliff and swam to her waiting boat to make her getaway. That's when she was spotted by two courageous women, who have asked to remain anonymous. They pursued her, overtook her on their own watercrafts—a pair of Sea-Doos—apprehended her, and held her until authorities arrived.

Larry hit the pause button again as he high-fived me, cheering, "That's my girl!"

"And in an astounding turn of events," Melanie said when Larry restarted the broadcast, "the same unidentified women managed to find the gold and what is believed to be a murder weapon linked to another homicide still under investigation."

It was my turn to hit the pause button. "If only I had a video of Sergeant Nussbaum's face when those officers dumped that bag of gold on the table," I laughed. "That would be nothing short of priceless." Time to let Melanie finish her story.

"I'm sure there'll be more information as law enforcement's and our own investigations continue, but for now, if we put the events in chronological order, this closing portion of my report will likely prove to be the first piece of the puzzle. According to military records, Corporal Henry Dixon was stationed in a region of South Korea known as Boseong. While Dixon was there, a gold statue of the mountain god Sanshin, made from 60 pounds of pure gold, disappeared from a Buddhist temple.

"Dixon is believed to have stolen the statue and hidden it while using every opportunity to pound the gold into smaller and smaller portions. Then, with the statue in unrecognizable pieces, he began stashing a few pounds at a time in packages he shipped home, hollowing out dolls and other figurines to hide his cargo.

"Mrs. Henry Dixon was said to have remarked that her husband seemed obsessed with Oriental dolls and statuary, but always sent a note with each one, telling her to store it away. Ignoring his instructions, she, instead, used their fireplace mantel to show off the dolls and statues she considered too pretty to hide.

"When Sergeant Dixon got back to his home in Alabama, he is said to have immediately swept the entire display into a duffel bag, slammed out the door, and returned the following morning without them. Apparently, this was when he removed all the gold and stored it in the cave in Swallow Canyon.

"And that, ladies and gentlemen, is what we know for now. A fascinating story, albeit an unfortunate one. We'll keep you updated. But I understand some good has come out of all this tragedy," Melanie said, segueing into reporter Carter Cameron's part of the newscast.

"That's right, Melanie," Carter said as the police station faded away and Simmons Chapel Community Church came into view. "When Reverend Pratt's truck was stolen, he was left with zero transportation. And this beloved pastor ..."—the camera angle widened to show Reverend Pratt standing to one side of the reporter as Carter placed one hand on the man's shoulder—"... only had liability insurance, which means there was no coverage to help with the purchase of a replacement." Carter then extended the microphone toward the pastor.

"I'm not so much concerned about that," the preacher began. "One of my church members has already loaned me a vehicle to use until I can get something else and, as I always say, the Lord will provide. My greater concern is for all the people involved in everything that led up to and followed the theft of my truck. These folks and their families need our prayers."

"Wise words from Reverend Victor Pratt," Carter said, turning the mic to himself. "But as Melanie said, despite so much tragedy, some good has come out of this." Carter made a waving motion and, seconds later, the camera captured the stunned look on Reverend Pratt's face as a shiny black Chevy pickup, complete with a giant red bow, turned into the church lot and pulled up directly beside him.

Cousin Dennis, owner of the biggest Chevy dealership around, opened the driver's door and stepped out, took a few quick strides to reach Reverend Pratt, pressed a set of keys into his hand, and disappeared from the camera. "I-I don't understand," the preacher stammered.

Carter cleared his throat and swiped at his eyes with his forearm. "Reverend Pratt," he said, his voice breaking, "I have the great pleasure of presenting you with this pickup truck on behalf of an anonymous donor. You'll find the paperwork on the passenger seat, including a sales receipt showing it's paid in full."

"And that's not all, Reverend Pratt," said Carter, sounding like a game show host. "If you'll take a look at this monitor ..." As he said this, the scene faded and the smiling face of Kai Washington came into view.

"So touching, Carter," she said, eyes sparkling. "But we aren't finished yet. If you'll follow me," she said, looking directly into the camera, "we're about to put the icing on this party cake."

Kai walked up a sidewalk and onto the porch of a neat vinyl-sided bungalow. "Turning again to the camera, she said, "I'm about to knock on this door. Let's see who's inside."

Kai rapped a couple times and the door swung open. Trish Pratt's eyes widened when she saw Kai and the cameraman behind her.

"What is this?" Trish said. "I'm sorry, but my husband isn't here. I thought he was supposed to meet y'all at the church. Please tell me that camera isn't on."

"Well, Mrs. Pratt," said Kai, "the camera is rolling, and we'd like to ask you to step outside for just one moment."

"Oh, my goodness," Trish said, patting her hair. "I don't even have shoes on."

"That's okay," Kai said. "We're all home folks here. This won't take a minute, but there's something out here we'd like you to see."

Reluctantly, Trish stepped out the door. She was wearing a

short-sleeved emerald green top and denim capris. Bare feet and all, she was as cute as a bug.

The camera swung away from Trish and Kai, and a silver Chevy Spark clad in a huge red bow, just as the truck had been, sat in the driveway. "Mrs. Pratt, on behalf of an anonymous donor, WEEE would like to present you with the keys to this Chevy Spark."

Kai held out the keys to Trish, who had one hand to her mouth and the other mopping tears from her face. "We know you're caring for your mom, and we don't want you stuck here without transportation whenever Reverend Pratt's away."

At this point, Larry's and my eyes were running like Niagara.

"I'm so happy," I sniffed, handing Larry a tissue as I blew into my own.

"That was a very selfless thing you and Millie did with your reward money," Larry said, squeezing my shoulder as he blotted his eyes. "And Dennis gave you a fantastic deal on those vehicles."

"Yeah, he did," I said. "They aren't brand new, but they're close. The Pratts should get a lot of good years out of them. And Hat, too," I added.

Hat's pickup was in our driveway. His ride to Grantham was going to be one he'd never forget.

Right then my phone dinged a response from Millie: "Best money we've ever spent." And Larry and I agreed wholeheartedly.

17

"What'd Jane say about her Sea-Doo?" Larry asked. "You told her we'd pay for the damages, right?"

"Of course I did," I responded. "But after I told her how it happened, she said she and Cliff wouldn't hear of it, and that she intended to see if their insurance covered ramming escaping gun-toting murderers."

"That should be a new one for their agent," Larry said.

"I'd count on it," I told him. "And in truth, the damage is pretty minimal. Nothing a little nose job won't fix. And …," I added. "Drum roll, please."

Larry used the index fingers of both hands to pound the table.

"Jane and Cliff are going to see what they can do to help Hat," I announced. "And, this next announcement calls for another drum roll."

Larry obliged.

"They want to help his parents," I finished, clapping my hands in my excitement.

"Fantastic!" Larry responded.

Thursday I slept in and woke to the smell of coffee and bacon. Larry was sitting on the screened porch, so I made myself a glass of iced tea and a bacon biscuit before joining him.

"I'm so glad you made breakfast," I told him, settling down beside him and leaning over to kiss his cheek. "I've got to get ready and head for WEEE pretty soon, and I didn't want to be on the air with my stomach growling."

"I aim to please, ma'am," Larry assured me.

An hour later, I reappeared in all my TV get-up and earned a whistle from Larry for my efforts.

"Down, boy," I teased. "I'll be back as soon as I can." And with that, I hopped in my car, waved, and started on my way.

Larry was standing on the driveway when I got back. "You ready to go?" he asked.

"I need to change clothes," I told him. "And give me a sec to call Millie. I'll be right out."

Another call beeped in as I was finishing up my conversation with Millie. "Let me see who this is and I'll talk to you later," I said, disconnecting from Millie and answering the other caller. "Hello."

The caller, who spoke perfect English, identified himself as Myung Min-Jun, an attorney in Seoul. His firm, he explained, had been authorized to handle the return of the recovered gold to South Korea and to pay the reward to the finders.

"Mr. Myung, I'm so grateful."

"As are we," he said. "Simply allow me to say 'thank you,' on behalf of all of South Korea. Knowing the fate of the Sanshin statue is very satisfying. Being able to have the gold returned to us is as well. You, and I understand, your cousin, Mrs. Caffee, have made this possible."

"You do know, though," I said, "that we weren't the ones who originally found the gold."

"Yes," Mr. Myung replied. "I have been informed of everything. The three people who discovered the gold had no intentions of returning it to South Korea. And the only one still living, this Barbara Jean Hyche, has no claim on the gold or the reward."

"I'm glad to hear that," I said.

"Yes, they found gold that did not belong to them. They hid the gold again, and then you and your cousin found it. I believe one of your sayings is, 'Finders, keepers,'" Mr. Myung continued. "It would also have been wrong for a murderer to profit from her crime."

"Yes," I agreed, "that would have been very wrong. And we're happy to know the gold is going back where it belongs. There is one more piece of the gold that you need to know about," I added. As I explained about Cooter and the catfish, Mr. Myung chuckled.

"It would seem a reward is in order for this Cooter also," said Mr. Myung. "If you can assist me in retrieving that piece of the statue, I will consult with my client about compensating Mr. Cooter. I'm sure they will be more than fair with what is offered.

"And who knows," Mr. Myung added, "there may be another catfish for Cooter to catch. The preliminary report from your authorities indicates as much as three ounces of the gold may be missing."

"Before you go, Mr. Myung," I added, "I wanted to ask you about a reward offered by a Mr. Yi."

"Ah, yes. The $50,000," said Mr. Myung. "Unfortunately, now that he is aware that the actual statue has been destroyed, Mr. Yi has withdrawn his offer. I am sorry."

"Oh, please don't apologize," I said. "I just had to ask."

"Understandable," Mr. Myung replied, "and wise. I did a bit of checking on you, and I read on your website: 'Don't be afraid to ask. The worst thing they can tell you is 'no'.'"

"Sorry it took me so long," I said to Larry, who had been impatiently waiting to take off for Fall Creek. "A Mr. Myung called from Seoul. As soon as their courier arrives and takes possession of the gold, $82,158.45, or whatever is five percent of the gold's exact market value on that day, will be wired into an account set up in my and Millie's name. That'll cover the huge debt we owe Cousin Dennis, with money to spare, even after we give 10 percent to our church."

"What about Hat's share in the treasure?" Larry asked.

"I didn't mention Hadley Vincent to Mr. Myung. Any taxes or other fees that end up coming out of the finder's fee will be taken from my and Millie's share. Hat shouldn't have to worry about all that. Millie and I plan to have a cashier's check made out to Grantham University, and that will take a big chunk of Hat's third of the money. But it'll cover all his basic expenses for this school year."

"Why, wife," Larry grinned, "that's mighty smart of you." He punctuated his high praise with a kiss on the tip of my nose.

"Thank you, sir," I responded.

Larry picked up a set of keys and jangled them in front of me. "You sure you don't want to drive the pickup?" he asked.

"No, I'd rather you did. I'll stick with the Hyundai. You lead, I'll follow. You do know how to get there, don't you?"

"I do," Larry answered. "Let's get this caravan moving."

As we rolled through Fall Creek Village, I was so thankful Larry was with me, even if we were in separate vehicles. The two-story brick buildings were in terrible shape, and parked and broken-down vehicles made it a tight squeeze for even one-way traffic, even though the street was designated as two-way. Clusters of young men stood in the street and sat on the hoods of some of the cars. Their glares as we drove by let us know our presence was unwelcome.

A bright green Malibu Classic had a cluster of at least six guys around it. The hood was up, the windows down, and music poured out at teeth-rattling decibels. In front of me, Larry's taillights came on and he stopped directly beside it.

"No, no, no," I said, frantically pounding the steering wheel. "Stay in the truck! Stay in the truck!" I wanted to put the window down and scream. But instead, I sent a text, "B safe. Keep moving."

Ignoring my warning, Larry hopped from the pickup and walked over to the gathering. I frantically prayed for his safety. When the music suddenly stopped, I let my window down the tiniest crack and listened.

"Naw, man," one young guy in his 20s said, "he already tried that."

"What about your plug wires?" Larry said. "Here, let me try something." Larry reached farther under the hood, clearly tinkering with something.

Whatever he did, the effect was immediate and pleasing. "That did it," the 20-ish guy said. "You really know your stuff, man." He and Larry locked hands in a manly handshake. "'Preciate it."

235

"No problem," Larry said. "I've got to take this truck to a friend's up the street. That's my wife behind me."

Several of the guys turned in my direction. One even threw up a hand in greeting.

"When I take care of that, we'll stop back by. I'd like to take a better look at your ride," Larry told him.

My husband never ceased to amaze me.

Larry stopped a half-block short of the Vincents' apartment, motioning for me to wedge into the space between two junked cars. I threw up both hands to let him know I was utterly clueless as to why he wanted me to park so far away, but I complied. He pulled ahead to the next open space, parked and walked back to meet me. He knew I didn't relish a stroll through the Village.

When Millie and I had brought Hat home, we'd dropped him in front of his family's apartment and kept going. With everything Hat had to tell them, we didn't figure it was the best time to make our introductions and, in truth, we weren't all that happy about being in the neighborhood.

Climbing from the Hyundai and checking all around me, I scurried toward Larry. "Why," I asked, "are we parking all the way down here? I would have felt more comfortable parking in their doorway."

"You wouldn't want Hat to see his truck, would you? Now we can say we're parked down the block, 'cause we are."

"You clever man, you," I said, squeezing his hand and hanging onto it. "I knew there was a reason I loved you."

"Only one reason?" Larry asked.

"Maybe a few more," I said. "As Daddy always says, I 'married a keeper'."

Several residents, seated on their stoops, stared toward the street. And toward us. I waved, but no one waved back. Children ran and played in the weedy yards, and several girls who looked barely old enough for training bras flirted brazenly with a group of teenage boys.

At D2, we mounted the stoop, knocked, and waited. A pretty grapevine wreath decorated the door and a cheery pot of begonias stood on either side of the stoop. Mrs. Vincent was making the best of her situation.

The door swung open and Hat, sporting a Grantham U cap, ushered us inside. "Nice to meet you, Mr. Bates," Hat said. "I feel like I already know you."

"Likewise," Larry returned. "And call me Larry. Larry and Judy."

"You know, until you said that," I said, addressing Larry, "I hadn't even realized he'd never called me anything. Unless you count 'old lady'," I teased.

"I never!" Hat said. "Well, maybe almost. I didn't know what to call you, so I sort of skated around it."

"Well, you do now," I said. "And this must be your mom."

A small woman with shoulder-length light brown hair stood behind Hat. "I'm Carla Vincent," she said, and this," she said, "is my husband Richard."

237

"Nice to meet you," Larry and I said in unison, as I shook Carla's hand and Larry stepped over to shake Richard's.

"You'll excuse me if I don't get up," Richard said.

"Richard," Carla scolded, "everyone's not comfortable with your little jokes."

"It's okay," Larry assured her.

"We really appreciate you giving Hadley a ride to …" He paused. "There it goes again. Help me, Mother."

"Grantham, honey," said Carla. "Richard is getting better all the time, but sometimes he has what we call his 'glitches'."

"Or CRC, as I call it," said Richard.

"What's CRC?" I asked, ignoring the warning looks from Larry, Carla, and Hat.

"Can't remember crap," Richard said.

We all five burst out laughing.

"We really do appreciate your kindness," Carla said. "When Hadley told us what he had done, well, we were simply appalled. Sneaking into other people's houses. Scaring the daylights out of you, Judy, and your cousin. Not telling us the truth about his truck. We raised our son better than that sort of behavior, didn't we, Richard?"

"We certainly did," Richard agreed.

"We're glad he's 'fessed up," I said. "And even if the circumstances were unusual, I am so thankful they led to my meeting your son. And my cousin Millie feels the very same way."

"We hope to meet her too," Carla said.

"She and I would love to come back for a visit," I said.

"That'd be so nice," Carla responded. "We don't get a lot of company these days."

"Hat, uh, Hadley," I instructed, "put my and Millie's cell phone numbers in your mom's phone." He'd already added them to his own. He lifted his mom's phone from an end table, wiggled his thumbs a few times, and announced, "Done."

"You haven't seen the last of us, I promise," I told Carla and Richard. "And neither has this kid of yours. For some reason, I've gotten quite attached to this little pain-in-the-neck."

Carla and Richard both smiled, clearly proud of their son. And who could blame them? I believed Hadley Vincent had a bright future ahead of him. And once Larry got to know him, I knew Larry would be as sure of that as I was.

"Guess we better be going," Larry said. "Richard, can I push you down the sidewalk to see your son off?"

"I can wheel myself," he said. "I'm becoming an old hat at maneuvering this piece of machinery." Realizing what he'd just said, he let out a chuckle. "Stands to reason I'd be 'old hat' since Hadley there is the new one."

Score another point for Richard's sense of humor, even if he'd probably meant "old pro." Hat's parents were super, and he seemed to have inherited all their good qualities. No wonder Millie and I had taken to him so easily.

Hat slung his gigantic duffel bag over his shoulder and held the door for the rest of us. Larry and I went out first and quickly moved to the sidewalk to make room for Richard's wheelchair on the tiny stoop. When Richard rolled to the edge, Larry gripped both sides of the chair and eased the front wheels onto the sidewalk.

"Beats jarring your teeth in that drop-off," Larry said, matter-of-factly. "The car's over here."

All five of us maneuvered down the sidewalk, Larry in the lead. As we passed the truck, he never slowed until he heard Hat's low whistle. "Now that's a ride," Hat said. "One of these days ..."

"Why not today?" Larry said, turning and pitching him the keys.

"Huh?" said Hat.

"Huh?" said Richard and Carla.

"Let me have that duffel," Larry said, as Hat stood like a deer in the headlights. When Larry tossed it into the back of the pickup, Hat dropped to his knees in total meltdown.

"Don't mess with me, man," Hat said, tears choking his voice.

"We'd never do that," I assured him. "You helped us recover the gold and we wanted you to have a dependable vehicle to drive while you finish your education."

"But you've already told me I'm sharing in the reward money," Hat sniffled through his tears. "This is coming out of that, right?"

"No, it isn't," I firmly told him. "Your part of the reward money is earmarked for this year's tuition, and what's left we'll talk about when the money's in hand. Now get in and drive yourself to Grantham."

"Y-you're for real?" he asked, still not believing.

"Like, totally," I said, taking his keys and pointing them toward the truck. "Presto, unlock-o," I said. "See, if the key fits, drive it."

Hat jumped to his feet, hugging me, hugging Larry, hugging his mom and then his dad. "I don't believe this," he said. Turning to his parents, he asked, "Did y'all know anything about this?"

"We're as stunned as you are," Carla said, tears coursing down her cheeks.

Richard sat, head down, also in tears. Larry and I couldn't stop grinning.

Cousin Dennis had told me this truck was "tricked out," meaning it had been customized with extra goodies that a young person would find highly appealing. Cousin Dennis had been right. Hat was over the moon.

"I still can't believe this," Hat said, sliding behind the wheel. Just as quickly, he was out again, making one more round of hugs and promising his parents he'd call as soon as he got to Grantham.

"And I said 'call,' not text," Carla reminded him.

"I will, Mom. I promise."

"Son, you drive careful," Richard said. "You know how your mom worries."

"Gotcha, Dad," Hat said. "Sure glad you don't." There was that family sense of humor again.

"Hang on," I said. "Photo op."

Hat stood between his parents with the truck as the backdrop. "Perfect," I said. "Now let me and Larry get a pic with you."

I showed Carla what to touch on my phone, and Larry and I moved into place on each side of Hat. Carla gave a thumbs-up and handed me my phone for inspection.

"Good pics," I said. "Now, a few of you in and around the truck," I said to Hat. He circled the truck, stopping at front, back, and sides. Then he was back in the driver's seat. He turned the key and the engine roared to life.

"Sweet," he said, grinning wider than me or Larry.

And at that moment, I took the sweetest picture ever.

The four of us watched as Hat pulled away from the curb and drove cautiously out of the Village. Then Larry, Carla, and I trailed behind Richard as he wheeled his way back to their apartment. Larry assisted Richard onto the stoop, and Richard pushed the door open and went inside on his own.

"He's doing more for himself all the time," said Carla, smiling. "No words …" She could get no further.

"Being able to do this has brought us far more joy than we've given," I told her. We left then, promising to return soon for a lengthier visit.

"Circle around and stop back by that Malibu," Larry reminded me. When we reached it, there were only two guys still out there.

This time, I let the window all the way down as I listened. "Hey," Larry said. "You got time for me to show you a couple things?"

"Sure, man," the car owner said. "Me and my li'l bro was just sayin' you wouldn't be back, and here you are."

Larry pointed at different things beneath the hood, speaking what to me was the foreign language of mechanic-ese. The car owner and his little brother apparently spoke it too, because they both nodded and pointed and rattled off terms like *torque* and *vapor lock.*

By the time we pulled away, Larry, Maurice, and Mackie had already made a date to meet at Terrell's garage. "They'll really like seeing all those classic cars, and Terrell and I can give them several ideas to help with their Malibu."

"Did I mention that I love you?" I asked, leaning over and kissing his cheek.

"Something like that," Larry answered.

Epilogue

Shortly after Larry and I returned home, my phone rang, and I saw it was Norway calling. "Hello," I said.

"Hello, Judy," my friend Iren Nordstrand said. "Have you enjoyed your lake time?"

"I have," I said sincerely. "How's everything in Kolbeinsvik?"

"Det star bra til," she said, meaning, *It's all good.* "The weather has been perfect. We hope it will continue while you are here."

Norway's weather is the ultimate in fickle. You could be enjoying a sunny 70 Fahrenheit one minute, and the next, the wind would pick up and the temp plummet to 45—and that was at the height of summer, the only time of year Larry and I chose to visit. I think Norway is one of the most beautiful countries in the world. Still, I'm a thin-skinned Alabamian who considers anything below 70 sweater weather.

"Per and I are making many plans for your visit," Iren said.

"And we are so looking forward to being there," I responded.

"I'm still amazed that Bill actually agreed to come—he's not big on flying—and Millie would never have said she'd come without him. Not as a fifth wheel."

"Fifth wheel?" Iren asked. "How many of you are coming?" she asked, concern creeping into her voice.

I laughed. "Sorry," I said. "American expression. Only the four of us are coming."

"Okay," she said, sounding relieved.

We tossed around some ideas for things to do and places we could go without turning our stay into a marathon. We both wanted Millie and Bill to see and experience as much as possible.

"We'll do a video chat next week when Larry and Per can talk too," I said. "Maybe even get Millie and Bill to join us."

"That would be good," Iren said.

"And we'll soon be landing in Bergen!" I said, referring to the city where our plane would touch down in Norway. From there, it was a half-hour ferry ride to Per and Iren's home in Kolbeinsvik.

"Are you flying through Amsterdam?" Iren asked. That was the usual route to many European destinations.

"Yes," I said. On our previous trip, I'd found a flight through London with a nine-hour layover. We'd flown through the night, gotten a decent amount of sleep, and arrived at Gatwick the next morning, catching the train for the 26-minute ride to Victoria Station. We'd used that time to see Buckingham Palace, indulge in tea and scones, and find a few bargains, including a Royal Bayreuth cup and saucer, my favorite in my growing collection.

This time, there would be no adventures before we got to Norway. Just the short, normal plane changes and layovers, first in Atlanta, then Amsterdam.

Or so I thought. But that is another story …

What's Real?

Chapter 1: Millie is my honest-to-goodness cousin and a very talented artist, although her studio and the family farm are totally fictitious. Her bout with cancer was very real, and I'm so thankful to say that she has been happy and healthy for many years since completing her treatments.

Lewis Smith Lake, or Smith Lake, as most people call it, is a manmade reservoir with over 550 miles of shoreline covering parts of three Alabama counties.

Fall Creek is imaginary, but the idea for it was based on Falls City, which really did exist before Smith Lake was formed. According to an article I found on the website www.FreeStateOfWinston.org, Falls City was pretty much a ghost town before the land was flooded in 1961. Sadly, historic preservation laws weren't in place at that time, so it's believed that many significant historical and archaeological sites dating back to the land's occupation by members of the Chickasaw and Cherokee tribes, and even earlier, were buried beneath the waters.

WEEE—"WEEE put the fun in television"—isn't a real TV station, but I was inspired to create it after all the years I spent doing guest appearances on WBRC Fox6 in Birmingham, Alabama.

Chapter 2: I am a true fan of DQ Blizzards, with their Turtle Pecan Cluster being my fave. I try to limit myself to only a few each year.

Chapter 3: Rock Ledge Marina isn't real, but it's based on Rock Creek Marina in Crane Hill, Alabama, where giant carp really do hang out and drink crackers from baby bottles. And yes, I really do let them suck crackers from between my toes! It's well worth a visit for the experience.

My wrecker operator, Adam, is married to my husband's niece, Ashley, and is the third generation of the Lyle family at Lyle Wrecker Service in Haleyville, Alabama. Without his expertise, I would probably have towed that truck out nose first.

Chapter 5: Chalybeate Springs, which is featured more in *A Bargain to Die For*, was the original name for the area that is now Gardendale, Alabama. I only recently learned that an unincorporated spot named Chalybeate Springs really does exist today in Lawrence County, Alabama. My imaginary town is located in Jefferson County, closer to Birmingham.

Faye Gilliam Busby is a real human being who won a contest I ran when *A Bargain to Die For* was released. She and I started second grade together and continued at the same school through ninth grade. We've remained friends ever since.

Chapter 7: Jackson Pollock was an American abstract impressionist painter, known for—believe it or not—taking household paints and pouring and splashing them on canvas. At a thrift store, a Costa Mesa, California resident paid $5 for what turned out to be one of his paintings. The last information I could find stated that she had turned down an offer of $9,000,000 from a Saudi art collector. I'm not that greedy. I'd have settled for half that!

Chapter 12: The shark-looking watercrafts Millie and I saw when we cruised by the Bartletts' mansion are Sea Breachers, water toys that can actually be submerged for short dives. They're amazing, and amazingly expensive. Read more about them and see videos of the Sea Breacher in action at www.SeaBreacher.com.

Questions & Contact

If you have a question about any person, place, or thing mentioned in this book that I haven't already explained here or elsewhere, feel free to email me at judywbates@bargainomics.com. And I'd love to hear your thoughts on this book.

Let me also remind you that I'm available for speaking engagements. Learn more and follow my bargain and Bible posts on www.Bargainomics.com and on my Facebook page, www.facebook.com/Bargainomics.

Coming Soon

When I wrote my first mystery, *A Bargain to Die For*, I had intended for Carrie Parker, my dad, and many of the other characters from that book to carry over into the next mystery. However, I felt compelled to change my plan. These people deserved their own series, where each could tell more of their own story. So, now I'm in the process of writing the first of what I hope will be the long-lived story of *Life in Chalybeate Springs*. I don't think it will be a mystery—at least, not in the traditional sense—but I believe it will be a delight. I hope you'll watch for it.

A Bargain to Die For

"Bates gets drawn into a mystery, along with her cousin and sidekick, artist Millie Caffee .... Cozy fans will be pleased."

(Publishers Weekly)

"A most enjoyable read. Humor and mayhem in just the right mix."

(Tim Hulsey, GoodReads.com)

"Such a creative and gifted storyteller. I loved the mystery. It grabbed my attention from the beginning and held it until the end."

(Gregory G. Hill, M.D., GoodReads.com)

"I am an avid reader. I read every day of my life. I don't normally read mysteries, but I thought I would give *A Bargain to Die For* a try since I am very familiar with Judy Woodward Bates through her web site and Facebook.... I absolutely loved the book! It was a page turner, and I had a hard time putting it down to even sleep! Most of the time, I was sitting on the edge of my seat."

(Jimmy M. Tucker, Amazon.com)

"*A Bargain to Die For* is very well written and thoroughly entertaining! It is so refreshing to read a good book that isn't R-rated or worse. I had a huge grin on my face by page 2! I can't wait for another book by Judy Woodward Bates!"

(BamaLady83, Amazon.com)

"I think we have another Anne George in the making. Go ahead and write us another book!"

(Mary Beth Clark Henderson, Amazon.com)

More Bargainomics

Visit my website at www.Bargainomics.com and follow me on Facebook and Twitter.

Search for the word *Bargainomics*.

And watch for another Bargainomics Lady mystery coming soon!

Made in United States
Orlando, FL
04 January 2022

12905742R00147